NEW YORK REVIEW BOOKS
CLASSICS

T0017219

A VERY OLD MAN

ITALO SVEVO (1861–1928), whose given name was Aron
Ettore Schmitz, was born in Trieste into a Jewish family of Italian
and German descent. Svevo published two novels in the 1890s,
A Life and *As a Man Grows Older* (available as an NYRB
Classic), but after they were dismissed by critics and ignored by
the public, he abandoned literature and went to work in his
father-in-law's paint business. He returned to writing only after
the young man whom he had hired to tutor him in English,
James Joyce, asked to see his novels and expressed admiration
for them. With Joyce's support, he published *Zeno's Conscience*
in 1923 to international acclaim. Svevo had finished a new
book (*The Tale of the Good Old Man and of the Lovely Young Girl*)
and was at work on another (published here as *A Very Old Man*)
when he was killed in a car crash.

FREDERIKA RANDALL (1948–2020) was a writer, reporter,
and translator. Among her translations are Ippolito Nievo's
Confessions of an Italian and, for NYRB, Guido Morselli's
The Communist and *Dissipatio H.G.* She received the National
Endowment for the Arts Literature Fellowship for Translation
and the PEN/Heim Translation Fund Grant, and with Sergio
Luzzatto, the Cundill Prize. She finished her translation of
A Very Old Man shortly before her death in Rome.

NATHANIEL RICH is the author of the novels *King Zeno*,
Odds Against Tomorrow, and *The Mayor's Tongue*. His translation
of *The Wrench* appears in *The Complete Works of Primo Levi*.

A VERY OLD MAN

ITALO SVEVO

Translated from the Italian by
FREDERIKA RANDALL

Introduction by
NATHANIEL RICH

NEW YORK REVIEW BOOKS

New York

THIS IS A NEW YORK REVIEW BOOK
PUBLISHED BY THE NEW YORK REVIEW OF BOOKS
435 Hudson Street, New York, NY 10014
www.nyrb.com

This book was translated in part thanks to a grant awarded by the Italian Ministry of Foreign Affairs and International Cooperation

Frederika Randall is grateful to the National Endowment for the Arts for a 2020 grant to support this translation.

Library of Congress Cataloging-in-Publication Data
Names: Svevo, Italo, 1861–1928, author. | Randall, Frederika, translator. | Rich, Nathaniel, 1980– writer of introduction.
Title: A very old man : stories / by Italo Svevo ; translated from the Italian by Frederika Randall ; introduction by Nathaniel Rich.
Description: New York : New York Review Books, [2021] | Series: New York Review Books classics | This is an original selection of short stories translated into English. It has no equivalent Italian edition. |
Identifiers: LCCN 2021004663 (print) | LCCN 2021004664 (ebook) | ISBN 9781681375939 (paperback) | ISBN 9781681375946 (ebook)
Subjects: LCSH: Svevo, Italo, 1861–1928—Translations into English. | LCGFT: Short stories.
Classification: LCC PQ4841.C482 V4713 2021 (print) | LCC PQ4841.C482 (ebook) | DDC 853/.912—dc23
LC record available at https://lccn.loc.gov/2021004663
LC ebook record available at https://lccn.loc.gov/2021004664

ISBN 978-1-68137-593-9
Available as an electronic book; ISBN 978-1-68137-594-6

Printed in the United States of America on acid-free paper.
10 9 8 7 6 5 4 3 2 1

CONTENTS

INTRODUCTION

"I AM A man born in inopportune times," says Zeno Cosini in *A Very Old Man*, a line thick with dramatic irony, since the description applies much better to his creator, Italo Svevo, for whom it could serve as an epitaph. In Zeno's case, the meaning of "inopportune" is narrow. As a young man, his elders didn't respect him. In the aftermath of World War I, having finally won senior status, Zeno discovers that the youth are not only running the world, but his own family business. He is left out again.

But Zeno's creator had it worse. Inopportunity in all its manifestations—bad timing, rotten luck, missed connections—is the dominant theme of Italo Svevo's life, work, and afterlife. Aron Ettore Schmitz was born of German and Italian descent in Trieste, itself a city of mixed parentage, the subject of a paternity dispute between Italy and the Austro-Hungarian Empire, and largely populated by Slovenians. Svevo spoke Triestine, a dialect that borrows from Slovenian, Greek, and German, and is unintelligible to other Italians. Although he wrote in formal Tuscan Italian, following national literary convention, it was for him a second language, and one he despaired of mastering. "Every Tuscan word we write," he says in *Zeno's Conscience*, "is a lie." Schmitz's cultural sensibility was neither Italian nor Triestine, however, but German. He attended boarding school in Swabia, where he was heavily influenced by the deterministic philosophy of Arthur Schopenhauer, and chose a pseudonym that reflected his mongrel identity ("Italo Svevo" means "Italian Swabian"). He was a Jew who converted to Catholicism to appease his wife, though only after receiving a dispensation for refusing to learn the catechism, leaving him in good standing in neither religion.

One of Italy's greatest authors spent most of his life too ashamed to admit he was a writer. He hid his passion from public view—he even avoided discussing it with his wife—while working for nearly two decades in the correspondence department of the local branch of the Union Bank of Vienna. During this period he wrote *Una Vita* (*A Life*), about the simmering desperation of white-collar life, and *Senilità* (*As a Man Grows Older*, a title suggested by Joyce), about an affair between a failed writer and a woman of dubious morals. The novels, quietly radical in their subversion of nineteenth-century literary convention, were published at his own expense and roundly ignored, apart from a couple of reviews that scolded him for his low subject matter. A fellow banker, upon later hearing that his colleague had published novels, exclaimed, "Who? Not that jerk Schmitz?"

For the second half of his professional life he worked for his father-in-law, manufacturing protective paint for ships' hulls. By his fortieth birthday he had renounced his literary aspirations. "The writer in him," wrote his wife, Liva, in her *Memoir of Italo Svevo*, "seemed fast asleep." He spent the next two decades, the prime of many novelists' careers, making varnish.

Svevo's one stroke of fortune was so extreme—one of the great lucky breaks in literary history—that in retrospect it seems only inevitable, only Svevian, that it should be followed by a final cruel thud of fate. In Svevo's life, as in his fiction, no pleasant surprise went unpunished.

When his firm opened a new factory in a London suburb, Svevo resolved to improve his poor command of English. He arranged for private lessons from a twenty-five-year-old Berlitz instructor who had developed the reputation, as Livia put it, of "a fashionable teacher of Trieste's rich bourgeoisie." Svevo called him "Professor Zois." For one lesson, James Joyce asked Svevo to critique the first three chapters of a novel that had stymied him; Svevo's homework assignment encouraged Joyce to finish *A Portrait of the Artist as a Young Man*. When Svevo admitted that he, too, had written fiction as a young man, Joyce read his novels within days. At their next lesson Joyce declared that Svevo had been unjustly neglected by his critics and was the most important Italian writer of his era. He recited passages of Svevo's fiction from memory.

Emboldened, the paint manufacturer returned to his private hobby. After the outbreak of World War I freed him of his professional obligations, he began a new novel. *La coscienza di Zeno* was published in 1923, three years after *Ulysses*. In Italy, *Zeno* enjoyed the same response as its predecessors. Belatedly, however, thanks to Joyce's enthusiastic advocacy to a cohort of influential Parisian critics, *Zeno* became a Continental phenomenon. His life, as Svevo put it, underwent a "revolution." He was celebrated at aristocratic literary salons in Paris and Versailles, hailed as "the Italian Proust," cheered in the streets of Milan, and mobbed by young artists and writers at his local café.

Thus began the most prolific—the only prolific—period of Svevo's life. For the next three years, Svevo tried to make up for lost time. He edited translations of his work, campaigned for the republication of *Senilità*, conducted a lively correspondence with editors and critics and patrons, lectured on Joyce, read Kafka and Proust, wrote new stories and plays, and, as early as January 1927, began a new novel about an old man named Giovanni Respiro. ("Respiro" is the first-person present tense form of *respirare*, "to breath easily again, as after a period of exertion or trouble.") In later drafts, Giovanni became Zeno Cosini, and Svevo accepted that he was writing a sequel.

His wife reports in her memoir that Svevo, approaching his seventieth birthday, "worked with a certain difficulty." He had experienced a series of heart problems and complained of weakness, worrying that a great "blow," usually imagined as a stroke, was coming for him. Nevertheless he managed to produce a manuscript of nearly book length by the time he died on September 13, 1928, following a minor automobile accident that overstrained his heart.

Like its author, *A Very Old Man* is stuck in between. It's neither a novel nor a story collection but a series of attempted openings, scenes, subplots, and character sketches. Livia retrieved the new Zeno fragments from a chaos of unsorted papers in his study and published them in a volume together with some of his short fiction. The collection was introduced by Svevo's most important Italian champion, the young poet and future Nobel laureate Eugenio Montale, who called Svevo "the greatest novelist our literature has produced from Verga's day to our own."

Yet in the century since, readers hoping for further encounters with Svevo's genius have typically turned to the earlier novels, with disappointing results. While *Una Vita* and *Senilità* were ahead of their time, they also lagged well behind *Zeno's Conscience*; the novels belong to the realist tradition that Svevo undermines, but does not fully escape, until his masterpiece. The audacious, indefatigable Frederika Randall, who completed this new translation shortly before her death, was right to identify *A Very Old Man* as *Zeno's* legitimate heir. The lineage extends well beyond the identity of the protagonist. The dark irony, self-flagellating introspection, manic obsessiveness, and unapologetic moral perversity—the qualities that make *Zeno* one of the most thrilling works of the twentieth century—cackle from every page.

A Very Old Man begins not long after *Zeno* ends. The war, which descends upon the Cosinis in *Zeno's* final pages, is over. Zeno, an inveterate gambler, has squandered his wartime profits through a hoarding scheme gone bad, but little else has changed, despite some chronological eccentricity that the author had yet to sort out. Zeno, depending on the chapter, is sixty-one or sixty-three or seventy; his son and daughter, young children when we last saw them, seem to have aged approximately two decades during the war. Beautiful Antonia has chosen a disappointing match in the dull Valentino, a union redeemed only by its blessing of a grandson, Umbertino, whose curiosity about the world brings Zeno back to his own youth. Zeno's son, Alfio, is a struggling painter, ripe with bohemian hauteur; as Zeno tries to navigate his disappointment about his son's artistic pursuits, he finds himself crudely impersonating his own father, whose paternal disapproval dominates the early pages of *Zeno's Conscience*. Zeno's business partner, old Olivi, has been replaced by his son, young Olivi. Zeno has a few new servants and a new mistress, but the Cosini milieu is largely the same: burgher-comfortable, intimate, and largely amicable, its routine disrupted only by Zeno's periodic paroxysms. Augusta, Zeno's wife, also remains constant: homely, predictable, skittish, faithful, and unwavering in her love for her undeserving husband.

The major shift comes within Zeno himself. Though he continues to speak of life in terms of a fatal disease, obsess over his health, and gleefully catastrophize ("when I see a mountain I always expect it to become a volcano"), his aged heart's not entirely in it. The old angst has dried up. Zeno is no longer imprisoned by his desires; now, instead, he finds himself "in a rather enjoyable state of freedom. . . . Long life cures all ailments." He even discovers that his accursed cigarette addiction, by inhibiting his appetite, has helped ward off his weight problems. In short, the miracle cure proscribed by Dr. S. on the opening page of *Zeno* has succeeded. The act of writing his autobiography has rejuvenated him.

Yet it is *only* his writing that feels alive. Rereading the diary entries that constitute *Zeno's Conscience*, Zeno concludes that his account of his life story is "the only important thing that has ever happened to me. . . . How alive that life is, and how definitively dead the part I didn't recount." He finds himself back in one of the recursive loops that define his character. He lives what he writes, writes what he lives, and loses sight of where one activity ends and the other begins. He's hit upon the premise—that literature is more honest, more *real*, than life itself—that helped launch the modern novel.

Readers of *A Very Old Man* will find themselves in the same position as Zeno—uncertain where his story begins, where it's going, or where it ends. This is a consolation, of sorts. It's impossible to know what shape the novel would have taken had Svevo's chauffeur never run the family car into a tree. Each previous edition, in Italian and in translation, has presented the chapters in different combinations. Given the Escher-like quality of Svevo's narrative style, a series of fragments, linked by the weak connective tissues of memory and free association, seems as appropriate a form as any for the novel to take. One could imagine it ending where it begins, like his former tutor's *Finnegans Wake*, or perhaps with a sudden arbitrary blow, such as a stroke—or a car crash. No unfinished novel in literary history has better claim to remaining unfinished. *A Very Old Man* delivers a particularly Svevian thrill: the joy of reuniting with a long-lost friend who, while older and wiser, still has a long life ahead of him.

—NATHANIEL RICH

A VERY OLD MAN

THE CONTRACT

I'VE NEVER quite understood how I came to be so idle at present, when during the war I was thought to be a pretty industrious fellow. There's my nephew Carlo—I talked it over with him, as it, too, bears on my health—who told me I did well to take it easy. I can get back to work when the next world war comes around, he says.

He does have a way with words, that young devil with his Argentine-Triestine patter. It's true, I was very busy during the war, and when peace came I couldn't get moving at all. Like a windmill when the wind's not blowing.

Let me try to recall.—If only I had slowed down sooner; I just didn't register the great revolution taking place. I welcomed the Italian soldiers on the streets, for I knew it meant this city of mine would finally emerge from its Middle Ages. But then I'd go to my office and conduct my business as if the Austrian troops were still there, and Austrian lassitude. And when communications with Italy were restored, I wrote a nice letter to old Olivi, who spent the war in Pisa. It was a perfectly innocent letter; you could see I expected that, when the war ended, things would continue just as if the war had gone on. Fate, I wrote, had decreed just what my poor father had deemed impossible: that I should become the master of my own affairs. I told Olivi how prosperous our firm had become, about the many deals I'd signed, and how much we'd earned. All this very calmly and without boasting. Words were unnecessary: the facts alone were enough to make him explode with rage. And in fact, he exploded.

When a few days later I learned he was dead, I thought my letter was to blame. But no, he died of the flu. I had somewhat bluntly suggested we let things continue as fate had disposed, allowing my father's last wishes to slip my mind, now that they were pretty much ancient history. I invited Olivi and his son to continue in my employ, but I told him I would remain the boss. He'd have a free hand to resume any of his old arrangements as he liked; I would take on the more important business, and of course I'd have absolute freedom too. He could deal with employee relations. I was pretty weary of all that, although I'd had very few employees during the war.

I'm not sure, but it might have been a good thing if I'd learned of old Olivi's death right off—rather than eight days after the fact. I wasn't keeping track of the dates, but it might have been convenient if he'd died a few days earlier.

All in all, my lack of attention was certainly to blame for my falling into that disastrous business. I kept thinking that the war was still on, when I knew full well that peace had broken out. But I was in a hurry to close an important deal, so that when Olivi came back he'd have reason to admire me. Had I known he was dead, I might have felt much more carefree.

All this to explain why a large number of railcars full of soap arrived in Trieste from Sicily. During the war, soap had been everyone's fondest desire, and especially the desire of those who hoped to make a profit on it. I procured it greedily and paid in cash. During the war, I was never in any hurry to sell. But as I was preparing to now, I discovered that Trieste didn't want soap. People were no longer used to it, apparently. And then something worse happened: from all over Italy I began to get offers of soap at a lower price than I'd paid. At this point I became rattled and realized that for the soap, too, this new thing, peace, had interfered. However, there might be a way out, I thought. My soap was already here in Trieste, while the competition was farther away. I prepared to ship my soap to Vienna to get it there first and sell it off. I still don't understand exactly why my soap was then impounded. The free movement of goods was, it seems, obstructed for two reasons: people urgently needed soap, and the ingredients didn't meet the requirements of certain Austrian laws that I, too, knew a little something about. Negotiations went on for several months. Finally my soap was freed, but in the meantime everyone had been able to stock up on that painfully slow-to-be-consumed product, and I had to sell it at a loss, and for Austrian kronen, which only came in when it was too late to exchange them. They were worth almost nothing. This last operation demolished just about all the profits I'd accumulated with such enterprise and good fortune during the war. It was hard to accept, and all the more so because the young Olivi, who had since shown up still wearing his sublieutenant's uniform, laughed out loud when he looked at my balance sheets, all my big earnings absorbed by that last unfortunate operation. He seemed to have nothing but contempt for wartime affairs, and one day he said he thought it was natural that those involved in war commerce should come to ruin in times of peace. "If I'd been in charge I'd have had them all shot, the ones doing business during the war." Then he thought for a moment and, unsmiling, said, "Apart from you, obviously."

War had made this shy young man quite bold. At first I was concerned. How would a fellow so thoroughly steeped in Bolshevism deal with my firm? He was constantly finding fault with the wealthy. He and his father had run to Italy with their Austrian stocks and bonds under their arms. Without even thinking about it he had gone to the trenches, and when they finally succeeded in destroying the enemy he suddenly realized he had destroyed his own property. He was quite resentful about it.

"And your father?" I ventured. "He was a businessman after all. Not like myself, a war-commerce man, or you, an army man."

"It didn't occur to him," Olivi sighed. "During the war, all he could think about was whether I was safe or not. Poor thing!"

"I, too, was waiting to hear from Florence, but I still looked after the business," said I triumphantly. "Sure, my capital didn't increase, thanks to the damned soap. But at least I didn't let it be destroyed."

"Nobody was shooting at members of your family," Olivi replied bitterly. "I was in the trenches." He seemed to resent that my daughter hadn't been down there with him. His Bolshevism notwithstanding,

Olivi was just like his father when it came to the business: watchful, shrewd, and hard-nosed. The employees had been spoiled by me, no Bolshevik. He set them right. He made them respect their shifts to the minute, and whenever he could he reduced their pay.

I soon realized that while I couldn't talk to him, I could trust him. He was a model of tireless activity. And so I began to take it very easy. There was, to begin with, that day I recall with shame, when absolutely nothing happened beyond a slight stirring in my soul, but I thought, "It elevates me more if I command—without having to govern." For a time, Olivi would hand me important letters to sign. I would sign them, after a moment's hesitation, with an expression that said, "Not bad." If I wanted to, I could redo these, and better, but so as not to fatigue myself I would sigh, and sign.

The only operation to which Olivi devoted no attention was the matter of the soap. The kronen still hadn't appeared, and one day I blurted out, "But can't we force those Viennese to do their duty? Didn't we win the war?" He laughed heartily, so heartily that I understood that I was not among those who'd won the war, and I blushed.

Now, I'm quite sensitive to a reproach like that. I said nothing because it took me a while to do the calculations and determine I was fifty-seven when the war began. The following day I asked him, "Do you think that if I'd volunteered to fight, they'd have accepted me as a general? Because I don't believe they would have taken me as a foot soldier."

He laughed. "Well, it's true that our generals came with all manner of qualifications."

He wasn't all that nasty. Less nasty than I, because the night before I'd practiced everything I intended to say to him. Quite unmoved by his genial reply, I added, "Even the rank of sublieutenant wouldn't have suited me. You need good legs for that position: both to advance, and to run away."

He didn't respond to this quip. Rather, he looked sad; he was remembering a time when they had to retreat. And he, too, was slow to react. It wasn't until the following day that he said to me, "People who know nothing of war believe that a good officer is the man who's good at organizing a charge. I believe I served my country by sharing my faith with the many during the retreat."

"It's a matter of legs," said I, unmoved. And then he got angry. Not with me—with others. Various commanders who'd taken credit for his merits. He even had it in for some who were at an even further remove, the dead, I mean. Heroes—they were called—because they were cheap: they cost but a tomb and some memorial words. While the living, who'd done so much, were neglected and, in order to survive, had to go to work for Signor Zeno Cosini.

I didn't catch his wisecrack right off, and didn't reply until the next day. "Nice that poor Zeno Cosini has to pay for all the heroes who somehow had the wits to survive."

His laugh was contemptuous. I raised my voice. "You were fighting for the many, not just for me. Right in this very neighborhood you'll find others who owe you just as much as I do."

Still, I was shy about raising my voice. I didn't like doing it. In the end, it was true that he had fought while I made money. But the worst was to come. This business of commanding versus governing soon left me knowing nothing of my business. Whenever I happened to offer some advice, I was quickly derided. My advice was terribly out of date. I referred to offices that must be consulted for approvals which were no longer in existence. "You think you're living in Albert the Bear's day," Olivi would mock me. Or I'd suggest something we used to do under the old system, and Olivi would tell me that in 1914 the Serbs had assassinated an archduke, and then a great many other things had happened, and my advice was now moot.

I was beginning to get thoroughly bored with the office. At times I would take days off. My attachment to procedure demanded I inform Olivi the evening before that I wouldn't be coming in the following day. "Be my guest," Olivi would say to me, "be my guest." And he'd laugh. It was his way of letting me know he was happy to see less of me.

Already, I was forcing myself to go to work. My constant hope was to catch Olivi out in some mistake, that he'd overlook some letter or interpret it wrongly, so I could demonstrate how important my presence was. He never gave me the pleasure. One time I thought I'd detected an error. "Don't you even know how to read a letter?" he said, and showed me proof I was wrong. Months after one such argument, I realized I had, after all, been in the right for once, but I'd been so intimidated by his self-assurance that I was unable to stand my ground.

And so, between the disputes in which I was wrong and those in which I was quite unjustly accused of being wrong, I ended up looking not like someone in command, but like an obstacle nobody paid attention to. The employees weren't disrespectful, but neither did they turn to me for instructions, even when Olivi was out. I pretended not to notice that instructions were needed, knowing that whatever instructions I might give I would end up being proved mistaken. I kept very, very quiet, happy that nobody asked me anything.

Then one fine day came the attack. That idiot son-in-law of mine (poor fellow, I'm sorry to call him that; I don't like to be disrespectful now that he's dead) was engaged by Olivi to negotiate a new contract with me. Business was bad. The firm had to be reorganized and new markets identified. Olivi was preparing to travel and study the situation and would be devoting himself wholly to this new task. He would need to be compensated on quite a different basis. He wanted a salary a bit higher than his present one and 50 percent of the profits.

My son-in-law gazed at me with that pale, fat, and somewhat shapeless face of his (I never understood how my daughter could have chosen him) and asked me to forgive him for being the one to bring me such a message. He had done it for a good cause. Better him than someone else.

I was indignant. The entire history of my relations with Olivi father and son flashed before my eyes. For many years the conditions laid down by my father had been respected. If they were to change now, I would be free to remove Olivi from his post and take over the firm myself. But all of a sudden I hesitated. Those days when the war had freed me from any restraints and I'd impetuously thrown myself into the business were long past. The diabolically clever Olivi had convinced everyone I was incompetent. He had even convinced me.

I imagined myself besieged by people asking me for instructions, to whom I could only say, "Ask Olivi!"

Nor was it true that my son-in-law Valentino had done me a favor in delivering the message. I knew he esteemed Olivi greatly; me, not so much. He was an agent for a large insurance company, and had tried to get me to take out a policy for our entire transport system. At a certain point he understood that, since I was hesitant (Olivi was keeping me in the dark), he was getting nowhere, so he turned to Olivi himself, and in the wink of an eye the policy was signed and— truth be told—at conditions far more advantageous for us than I'd ever dreamed we could get. Valentino apologized to me, saying, "But you didn't explain this point to me, or that other thing..." In short, he offered Olivi better conditions than he'd offered me, and further- more—this was the worst part—his esteem for Olivi soared.

So he'd been wrong to accept the messenger role. I rejected all the conditions and asked Valentino to tell Olivi he'd been fired, that I would replace him with someone else if I didn't take over his job myself.

Now Valentino, like so many businessmen, believed that everything in this world can be discussed. What he didn't know was that my reputation in his eyes mattered more to me than how Olivi's reaction would affect my interests. He began to speak of the man's long service with the firm and his great experience. He had a disagreeable voice, poor Valentino. His large nose helped to shape the sound of it. And it wasn't a strong voice (what *was* strong in him?), so that the mo- notony of listening to him was compounded by the effort one had to make to catch what he said. I made the effort, then shut my ears so as not to hear words that meant nothing to me. Poor thing, he was dis- cussing my interests when what mattered was something else entirely.

At last he finished. He stood to leave and join the others, and before he went out apologized for having bothered me. I turned af- fectionate then, recalling that if there was someone to reproach it was Olivi, not Valentino. I smiled, thanked him, walked him to the door. He couldn't have guessed the vituperation seething in my soul, as it so often does. "What a good man I am!" I thought. "What a good man!" And I continue to be good, all evidence to the contrary. May poor dead Valentino forgive me, but instead of smiling at him, I'd have liked to have sped his departure with a kick.

I went to see the attorney Bitonti, son of my father's attorney. A man my own age, more decrepit than I, thin, with a small face framed by a white beard; his eyes, however, were lively and at peace. It's odd how certain people, when they consider a particular matter, see nothing else. Their entire person disappears, along with that of their interlocutor, and only the matter remains. He knew nothing of my case but what I told him, I, who was unable to keep only that matter in mind. He therefore risked getting lost along with me. But he limited himself to the matter, as ill-understood, ill-perceived, and poorly presented as it was. "You say that in wartime you were able to run your business by yourself," he said to me. "Now you must see if you can run it alone in times of peace. You say you're at least as important as Olivi in the office. Now you must determine whether you'll still be that important without Olivi. I don't think you should immediately replace the man. You must take charge of the firm yourself, and then begin to look for someone to assist or replace you."

I left, detesting him, but not letting him see it. Luckily! After spending some time with my gramophone—full of sympathy for myself, the liveliest sympathy—I finally saw that my poor self had but two choices. I could take on the job, doubtful that I would succeed, or I could give in to Olivi.

And that was when I decided to turn to Augusta for advice. Not that I thought she'd know what to do. But speaking to her would help clarify my ideas. At first she seemed even less helpful than I'd imagined. "But aren't you the boss?" she said. "How dare he do this? How dare he?" Devoting myself to the question of how Olivi had *dared* struck me as a magnificent waste of my time. Somewhat impatient, I went back to my gramophone.

I wouldn't have pursued the matter with Augusta if the next day, after we'd had luncheon and were sitting by ourselves, she hadn't asked, "So then, what have you decided?"

I told her I thought it was not unfair to give Olivi 50 percent of the profits. Which in those days weren't very much, not compared to our prewar earnings or those I was able to bring in during the war. Right now, Olivi and I should be dedicating ourselves to rebuilding the firm on a new basis. But if I was to be part of this, shouldn't I receive the same salary as Olivi?

It was easy to decide to tell Augusta all. That idiot Olivi, in talking to Valentino, who in turn told his wife everything, who in her turn had no secrets from her mother, had already forced me to be absolutely candid.

Augusta suggested I request double Olivi's salary. I solemnly agreed, though I already knew I wouldn't ask Olivi for so much.

In a desperate effort to distance Valentino from the talks, I decided to deal directly with Olivi.

He didn't seem embarrassed in the least. He treated the matter as offhandedly as if it were a question of agreeing or not to sell a shipment of goods. I, meanwhile, was hard-pressed to behave so casually. I smiled, I thought, and I argued, but all the same it was evident I was like the dog that stiffens when an enemy approaches, thrusting its tail between its legs. I was breathless, feeling the weight of the moment. Seeing him so sure and nonchalant discussing such an affair and feeling myself unhappy and insecure, I sensed how superior he was and decided I must keep him in the firm at all costs.

I proposed I be given a salary equal to his and that the profits should be shared, or else that we should skip settling on a salary for either of us and simply share the profits. It seemed to me I'd made a single proposal, but that wasn't how it seemed to Olivi. First he told me he was about to get married and that if he accepted my proposal he could see, from the previous balance sheet, the money wouldn't be enough for him and his family to live a decent life: he needed his full salary and half the profits, undiminished by any fee for me.

"But," said I, "if I'm not going to be paid for my work, then I'm not going to work. I'll pop in from time to time and look things over, sure, but I won't touch a pen."

Hypocritically Olivi said, "I'll be sorry to have to do without you, but there's no way around it."

It was the words that were hypocritical, not his stubborn approach, which meant: The participation you're offering isn't worth a penny.

I still had a little resistance in me. So I solemnly asked, "When must I give you an answer?"

He explained that eight days had already elapsed since he'd sent me his first proposal. And that he would have been happy to wait until the balance sheets closed at the end of the month, as per the old contract, but he was unable to do so because the party he was dealing with required a rapid reply. He needed my answer the following morning. He would be frank. He had shown my son-in-law Valentino a letter from some people who wanted to employ him on the same conditions he was asking of me. My son-in-law would let me see it that very evening.

This gave me a start, for two reasons. Olivi was letting me know that if I didn't come to an agreement with him he would strike out as my competitor, and further (and this was the more painful), once again a family member had been admitted to these discussions which—all the evidence now pointed to it—could only end in my defeat.

"But why did you allow outsiders to come between us?" I stammered.

"Outsiders?" he laughed. "Isn't he your son-in-law?"

I had to agree. "Yes, he is," I murmured. So here was another thing we couldn't talk about. It was enough to make my head spin. Olivi always had the better of me.

I didn't dare to continue talking about it, but again, and for the last time, played the role that Augusta—and she alone—had advised. The master. The boss.

"All right then. Tomorrow morning I'll give you my reply."

The strange thing was that I left the office immediately—the first time I'd done so just as the mail was being opened. At that hour in that season, being in the warm office was much preferable to being in the open air, under a thick bank of clouds threatening snow. I was behaving like the master—that is, master of myself—although not master of the office where the real master, Olivi, had stayed to work and would be nice and warm, while I had to scuttle about and find shelter.

I climbed up to my villa on foot. There was no sense in concealing my defeat from Augusta, given that Valentino would learn of it. I told her straightaway. In order to free myself from the weight of it, I had to tear her away from her household duties and her bath. It was true, I was no longer fit to work, I confessed. Maybe it was my age? I was just sixty-three, but mine might be a case of premature aging. Now, this was the very the first time that condition was mentioned in the family. When it later struck Valentino, I felt an instant of remorse, as if I'd infected him myself.

Tears came to my eyes as I spoke of my irrevocable old age. Augusta began to console me; she was so moved that she, too, was close to tears. She cares about money deeply, and she spends a lot, wisely so, in the sense that she doesn't worry about expenses when it comes to enhancing her own comfort. But I don't believe she was curious about what financial damage the new contract might cause. She assumed it would be small and saw it as just one more reason to console me.

And in fact it was small. The damage would grow worse if there were losses, because on top of absorbing the losses I would have to pay Olivi's salary: under the new contract he was exonerated from any losses because, in his opinion, the working partner of a firm should never have his salary reduced. It was, in short, a well-designed contract—from Olivi's point of view. But let me say immediately that although the contract strongly favored Olivi, after seven years of its terms I can't say I've been greatly damaged, except for my health (as I'll explain). Some years, the balances were splendid and our biggest problem was how to outwit the tax officials. Other seasons were less rewarding, but we never lost money. Overall, Olivi dealt with my business just as his father had, except that he earned more. A true sign of the times.

That first morning, after I'd endured the cold and my dejection, I stayed at home. I hadn't yet determined that I would never see my office again. I thought I was there to consider how to receive Valentino so as to preserve my dignity when he came by to see me, as he certainly would that evening. Actually, I didn't consider that question at all. I've no idea how to direct my attention where I want it to go. It's utterly independent of me. I recall that all day I was paralyzed thinking whether in the morning I ought to accept Olivi's proposal right off or whether I wouldn't do better to tell him to go to the devil and take over the business myself. The truth is, my thoughts always turn to the past, as if to correct it—well, falsify it—rather than to the future, where the absence of any formed plan makes it difficult to settle in.

And so when poor Valentino finally appeared, the best I could do was send him away (when I see a mountain I always expect it to become a volcano), telling him I'd just seen Olivi and we had agreed on the terms. Valentino looked baffled, then doubtful. He stared hard at me, investigating with that eye of his so sadly (for him) unacquainted with solemnity. Then he told me why he was dubious: he had seen Olivi at six that evening and it was now only eight. Therefore, he didn't see how I could have met him and discussed such an important matter.

I heartily dislike lying, and being forced to lie was yet one more reason to resent poor Valentino. And I really was forced, from the moment I told that first lie. But why was he so insistent? Later, when he died, I understood, and forgave him. He was just made like that: he couldn't drop a subject until he'd got to the bottom of it, and that occupied a great deal of time, because he thought slowly and very meticulously.

I told him I'd run into Olivi by chance on the street and we'd quickly reached an agreement. The matter wasn't so very important. I generously revealed the petty total of our profits the previous year. In short, it was of no importance to me or to Olivi, who was very much poorer than I.

Up to this point I'd been able to suppress that rowdy voice howling at me from deep in my gut, "What a good man you are, what a good man!" But apparently that howl escaped my lips and was detected by poor Valentino. In any case he took advantage of my good nature. He tried to tell me the matter was of great importance because if there were great losses one year, the payout of Olivi's salary would worsen my position.

And if so, what of it? Why, now that he'd heard that we'd reached an agreement (although he didn't believe it), was he suddenly putting forth arguments against agreeing? Was it to be sure he understood perfectly? I had no idea how he could have detected my inward fury and impatience, for I spoke only the calmest of words to him. I knew my firm and my business, and I was certain that we would see no losses with someone as prudent as Olivi in charge. Nevertheless, my fretfulness and my ire must have been evident and quite offensive, because all of a sudden poor Valentino's usual face—expressionless and rapt as a model employee's—drained of color and began to twitch as he made for the door. He was so upset it looked as if he would abandon all decorum and leave without a word. Then he paused in the doorway and said in a shaky voice (his amplifying nose notwithstanding), "Well, this business has nothing to do with me. I spoke only because Olivi asked me to and because it's in your interests."

Slouched in my armchair, I stared at him amazed, searching for something that could have injured him among the words I'd said. But nothing came to mind, and I was confused by his show of fine manners; he said we'd have dinner again and speak of many things, but never again of that affair.

Never again? Wasn't that a bit excessive? With so many things on my mind in that one instant, I was unable to locate the offensive word that must have escaped my lips. Perhaps he was more offended by the sound than the meaning of the words.

The hours that followed were peculiarly anxious ones. First of all I had to warn Augusta not to tell Valentino that I'd been at home for hours, or he would know I hadn't seen Olivi that evening. But how was I to do this, when Augusta would surely be in the sitting room with Valentino and Antonia? Then I had to find Olivi that same evening and come to terms immediately, before he saw Valentino again. There I stood, in utter distress, ready to go out in my hat and winter coat, the house as usual overheated because that was how Augusta preferred it, in the doorway of my study, undecided for several minutes whether to call Augusta or go to the Palazzo del Tergesteo where I knew I could still find Olivi, who never left work—in this he was like his father—until 9 p.m.

Just then Renata, little Umbertino's nursemaid, came by. She could help. I called out. She raised her dark eyes, astonished and a little frightened because it was the first time I'd ever addressed her when Umbertino wasn't with her, while I, although quite agitated, could not help but be stunned by the sight of her long and still somewhat childish legs, barely hidden by a pair of silk stockings.

It was a bit difficult to explain. I wanted her to get Augusta to come to me without revealing it was I who wanted her.

She understood immediately. She had a voice that broke on a shrill high note and then rose when, as now, laughter interrupted her words. A voice full of notes. "Signora Augusta sent me here to look for her glasses," she said. "I found them, but I'll tell her I didn't, and I'm sure she'll come to look for herself."

I wasn't at all sure things would work out that way, but in my doubt I let Renata go. When Augusta hurried in, though, I quite admired the girl's cleverness.

Fortunately, Augusta had not yet said anything to compromise me with Valentino. Nor was she at all surprised by the lie I'd told, she understood and even seemed to approve. It now seems odd to me, but I think I can explain her approval: she was annoyed just then at poor Valentino because he'd quarreled with our son Alfio. Naturally she agreed that I should go out and find Olivi and inform him that I'd already accepted the contract (long before my son-in-law got involved), and she would also tell Valentino that I'd undertaken an errand for her. Otherwise I couldn't have used the car, which could be heard up and down the neighborhood when taken out of the garage.

I found Olivi at the Tergesteo. I must have made a strange impression on him. I was behaving as if I was altogether inferior to him, my own employee. There was no time to think, I was in a hurry, and I abandoned myself to my obsession: eliminating my son-in-law from that discussion forever.

I said I was ready to accept all his terms on the condition he grant me a single concession, just one.

Olivi looked hesitant. He began to speak, slowly, the way he always spoke about business, with that mindless respect he brought to it, as if business had any significance beyond the money one could obtain from it, as if it were science, art, or invention.

And though I was behaving like a capricious child, I felt I was immensely superior to Olivi just then. He was trying, solemnly and laboriously, to tell me something I wasn't the least bit interested in and didn't want to discuss. He began very gravely, saying that he'd thought at length about his terms and therefore couldn't consider any modifications.

"And I don't propose any. What I want is something quite different," I shouted impatiently. I wanted to prevent Valentino from thinking he'd been instrumental in forging our agreement. Olivi couldn't hide his surprise. He'd known me for many years, but he'd never seen me behave so irrationally. He stared hard at me to be sure this was not a joke. He wasn't sure, he would never be—but what difference did it make in the end? Even supposing we decided the matter while I was deep in the grip of pure madness, it wasn't his place to choose this moment to hesitate. Thinking about it, he murmured, "It was I who asked Signor Valentino to speak to you. He seemed to be the most suitable man for the negotiation, because he's an old friend of mine and also one of your boys." Then, again in a murmur, he said, "Here's what we can do. I saw Valentino at six and I can easily say I met you on the street at seven." This is how one persuades those who reason too slowly, by speaking one's thoughts aloud. And then he said something very strange: "But now that I gather that Valentino isn't one of your boys..."

"He is my boy, but I don't want to appear to be a man who lets himself be commanded by his own sons." Although I said so unhesitatingly, Olivi's peculiar lapsus left me with a heavy heart. Was I not acting quite indelicately toward my son-in-law, who had never failed to show respect for me, and therefore also toward my daughter Antonia?

This suspicion stayed with me for a long time, and made my unhappy position even harder, after I had agreed to that contract depriving me of any role and not a little money. At times, in order to regain my peace of mind, I would become enraged with poor Valentino, whose involvement had forced me to sign the agreement so precipitously.

When Valentino was on his deathbed (and not before) my remorse finally became apparent, and it made me feel very unhappy. Olivi had kept his word with his usual seriousness, and Valentino never learned of the bad deed I had done him. It was just for that reason that I—with the typical cowardice of us misbelievers, who when we see someone dying imagine that on arrival in the afterlife they'll learn everything—wanted to confess to him and ask forgiveness for that deed, and also for some others I'd committed (for example some words I'd said against him to his wife, Antonia, who hadn't been moved by them, however). But they never left me alone with him. He was already quite hard of hearing, and though I was willing to make a confession to one man abandoning me definitively, I was not prepared to do so before many who would stay on to deride and reproach me.

I must admit—here I do confess—that I never held Valentino in great affection. I don't think it could have been otherwise, because he was very ugly—corpulent around the waist, short legs—worsening my stock, I felt. And so, beyond the really quite bearable remorse I felt at his deathbed, I was fairly cool and able to observe all with a calm eye. It seemed to me that all his visitors were more eager to confess than he was, despite the urging of his very religious wife. I fear this happens rather frequently where the dying are concerned.

Augusta, although she took part in the ruse against Valentino, never suffered from remorse.

That evening when I returned home, alone with me for a moment, she asked like a real accomplice, "Were you able to speak to Olivi and come to an agreement?" And when I nodded affirmatively, she heaved a sigh of relief.

The night that followed I was very uneasy. I couldn't even figure out which of my doubts—there were many—had been transformed into a nightmare, but something was weighing on me horrendously. Was it the contract itself? My sentence of terminal inertia? I thought, "If I'm worth anything in business, I'll end up finding something to do that suits me." But even this certainty did not give me peace.

After a couple of uneasy hours, I couldn't bear it anymore and I got Augusta up. She insisted I take a tranquilizer. The first effect of this remedy was to make me talk: "It's that damned contract that won't let me sleep, and further, I fear Olivi will tell Valentino that it was precisely his intervention that forced me to agree." I didn't say exactly what I was thinking because, I reckon, I already knew that this empty fellow, so replete with seriousness, would keep his word.

Augusta was not much help. She was quite blind where I was concerned, she believed that in any case I was really still the boss, and the following day when we went to the notary to sign the contract she suggested I withhold my signature because the document no longer pleased me. Little did she know that I was already familiar with all the clauses therein, including some that were fairly humiliating for me, and had accepted them all. "If Valentino hadn't put his nose in it the contract would never have been so quickly accepted, but now it's no longer possible to back out," I said.

Following those words, I found some peace that night. I'd discovered a way to attribute to Valentino wrongs that compensated for my own.

The signing proved painful, however. I knew all the clauses of that contract, but when the notary read them out one by one, they all sounded new to me. One stipulated that I was free to offer advice about the business, but that Olivi was equally free to accept or reject it.

I signed quickly. For all I knew there was a clause condemning me to death, because I stopped listening after the one that prohibited me from even thinking about my own affairs. I thought instead about Olivi and the hateful maneuver he had carried out, so deeply injuring a poor old man like me. The conflict was over. Which was why I now felt so weak and unarmed. Given how feeble I was and how strong my adversary, I thought I was in the right. A poor victim finally in the right. The feeling that I was a poor innocent victim would stay with me for a long time and deteriorate into illness, and it was born right there, when I had to endure the reading of that contract.

Afterwards, I wanted to run away. I felt I must get far from Olivi, to fortify my thinking in solitude and strengthen my revenge. Strange, the fury to distance myself in order to prepare to punish him.

But I hadn't prepared the words I wanted to say to him, I wasn't prepared at all. Having signed, and wanting to get away immediately, I instinctively held out my hand to Olivi, like a gentleman's obliged to do when he's been beaten at cards. And also when he suspects he's been cheated but doesn't have the proof.

Olivi shook my hand and said, "You'll see, Signor Zeno. You'll never have reason to regret signing this contract. In good time I hope to return your firm, not to its former luster, because we'll never have that kind of business again, but to a regular, orderly activity that will assure your existence."

His fine words didn't appease me at all. What did I care about a little less or little more income? They were tossing me out of an office where I'd been exceedingly happy—so long as Austria had freed me from my two bosses—and now they wanted to console me. It was too much.

In a strangled voice I said, "There are things that didn't belong in that contract. No, I mean it! You should have kept in mind that you were dealing with an old man who, obeying the laws of nature, would soon have given up his business. That clause that just barely permits me to open my mouth when I want some transaction to be pursued, or something else passed over, should be struck out."

The notary jumped to his feet, frightened. To tell the truth, I don't recall him; I didn't see him. I know that in that important seat sat something very young, fair-haired or redheaded, far livelier than one imagines a notary could be. I was struck by the gold frame of his glasses, on a gold chain that went behind his ear and into a buttonhole on his suit vest. Perhaps I noticed that chain because it was so pedantically orderly—the only thing about the man that really belonged on a notary, I thought.

He raised his voice. "But the contract is already signed and sealed. I don't see how you can think of changing it."

Olivi now intervened, grave-voiced and very calm, with all the quiet menace that someone in a very strong position and very sure of himself can convey. "The tax seals aren't important," he said. "In fact I only gave you time to reflect until eight in the morning yesterday. But it doesn't matter. I can always find other partners who I know are ready to sign this very contract. If you wish, Signor Zeno, we can tear up our agreement. I don't care. I'll give you back all your freedom. I only require that I am also granted my freedom today, immediately. From today I will never set foot in your office again."

My head was spinning. I'd been trying to resign myself to losing that office. And then from one minute to the next I was to have it back complete, with all the boredom, the responsibilities, and so much servitude. How, from one minute to the next, did I end up in that utterly new position? It wasn't an option, that was immediately clear. Seeing Olivi, who looked very decisive, was approaching the table where the contract lay, maybe to tear it up, I shouted, "The contract has already been signed and it's up to you, Signor Notary, to guard it. I never proposed to annul it." And here I tried to laugh, in order to stop and think what I wanted to say next. I tried. A victorious shriek issued from my mouth: "I simply wanted to say that you didn't negotiate with an old man as you should have. You could have obtained the same result leaving out some of those clauses. I don't give a damn about striking them out. The evil was already done when I learned you had even thought of them. Irrevocably."

Olivi was brusque and sure of himself. "There was no alternative. Believe me, Signor Zeno."

"So be it," I said. "We won't speak of it again." I was ready to leave. But then I retraced my steps to shake the notary's hand, and, once again, Olivi's. What the hell! Was one or was one not a gentleman? When I took Olivi's hand, however, I let it drop immediately, as if I'd been scorched. A gentleman mustn't feign a friendship he doesn't feel.

I left quickly because Olivi seemed to want to accompany me. And

I wanted to be alone. At times when I've been subject to someone else's force, solitude has often allowed me to get my balance, console myself, regain my confidence. Who knew? Maybe when I reconsidered it, my situation would appear less grim.

Outside the weather was unpleasant. Rain was falling on and off, light rain. The atmosphere was gloomy and heavy with humidity. What a bore! I yawned as I made my way, umbrella shut, down the gray street. At that hour the mail should have arrived in the office. I hesitated for a moment wondering if I should go, get there before Olivi did, and behave like the boss, opening the mail. I thought the idea was so original that I turned around, ready to walk back up the street. Then I changed my mind. Hadn't I made it clear that if I wasn't to be paid, I wouldn't work? Now I began to run in the other direction, fearful that I'd come too close to the notary's office and might run into Olivi again. And as I speeded up I had a strange thought: "My God! I'm already doing something."

How I adored activity at that moment. Especially the activity typical of that hour. How marvelous it was to open the mail! You removed a sheet of paper from an envelope and there was no way to predict what it concerned. The expectation was delightful, but very often followed by boredom or fury. True, after ten or so letters I usually couldn't take it anymore and left the rest to Olivi. Nevertheless, I'd had my fun.

Still walking in the direction of the sea, I decided not to tell Augusta right away that I didn't intend to set foot in the office again. It would mean confessing that with that contract, I'd been booted out of my own business. First I'd find something to do outside the house. Then I'd tell her that I couldn't stand the sight of Olivi, and therefore wouldn't be visiting the office anymore.

Meanwhile I had to get out of the rain, and so I headed toward the Tergesteo. But then I ran into Cantari, a salesman for the German factories making chemical products. I wasn't happy, because he sometimes met Augusta, and he might tell her he'd seen me out and about. After we'd exchanged greetings, I was keen to move on, but he wanted to stop and speak to me. He'd been asked by Olivi to let him know the prices of the chemical products he represented, and he wanted to know whether, by communicating those prices to me, he could save himself a walk across town to Olivi in the rain.

I told him that I didn't think that Olivi would be able to deal in chemical products. I knew the damn fellow was considering producing every article in this world, to replace those that, under the new order of things in Trieste, were no longer allowed to be sold here. I showed my contempt, which came naturally when I thought of Olivi. I didn't want to hear about chemical products.

And so the big fellow, so appreciated by Olivi because he never mislaid papers or forgot to visit clients or to deliver the necessary communications—a man of order, in short, because his profession demanded order and nothing else—cocked his umbrella and, resigned, set off.

In the meantime, though, I had changed my mind. Why add to my chagrin the discomfiture and the effort, the pain really, of deceiving Augusta? What did it matter that Augusta might suspect they'd managed to throw me out of my own office? The truth could be partially concealed. I could tell her, the first time I returned home early, that I'd had a violent headache. It would be easy to mimic any sort of illness that day. Augusta would surely oblige me to take a purgative. But maybe I needed one; I'd been made to swallow so much that was indigestible.

Shut up in my study after having given Augusta my explanation (result: I now had my head bandaged), I asked myself, "What will I do now?" I would perhaps find something to occupy me, books, or the gramophone. With a great deal of time on my hands, I might even make the great resolution to pick up the violin again. But how could I busy myself with such things when I was quarreling with Olivi? I hadn't yet delivered all the insults at my disposal.

Many days after the contract was signed, I realized that if old Olivi hadn't died I'd never have had to endure such an affront, because he wouldn't have permitted it. Such a reproach would of course have pained young Olivi, so respectful of his father's memory. Another thing I could have told him was that if my father had known what sort of people that stock of theirs would produce, he wouldn't have put the company in their hands.

I then studied the contract, of which I had a copy. It was written with diabolical cunning! Every clause took aim at my rights. One stipulated that if the firm were to close at my instigation, I stood to lose half my capital to Olivi.

That clause enraged me so much that I couldn't resist doing something about it, and so I reproached Valentino for his part in sealing the contract. I felt I could make that complaint in good conscience because I knew that he was responsible for the haste with which it had been signed. But he became angry, insisting he'd proposed we discuss the matter clause by clause, but I had refused, saying I'd already accepted the entire contract as one and inseparable. Those were his exact words.

I tried not to remember, but this wasn't possible because there'd been witnesses, and once again I had to stand down in defeat.

There was another thing that weakened my position for several days. My son Alfio, the painter, briefly had doubts about whether he would succeed at painting his peculiar pictures, and began to cast around in search of another occupation. Among other things, he considered devoting himself to business and thought of becoming partners with Olivi. But then he discovered there was a clause in the contract expressly forbidding him to do so. "But we inherited the firm from Grandfather," he groused, "and you should never have let it be touched." Showing respect has never been Alfio's strong point.

I then spent a few days thinking about what concessions I could offer Olivi in return for allowing Alfio to play a role. I concluded I would have to buy that permission with a sizeable sum of money. Meanwhile, though, Alfio had changed his mind and gone back to dirtying innumerable sheets of paper with tempera. But now I felt I owed him something, and that made me even more obsequious in my already difficult relations with my son.

Then one day I was mortified to learn that completely outside the contract, indeed quite contrary to all its precautions, Olivi had agreed to grant an important concession to Valentino. My son-in-law was to spend an hour each evening in the office to review the orders in the register and compare them with the original documents. On my behalf!

THE CONFESSIONS OF A VERY OLD MAN

April 4, 1928

A NEW ERA began for me on this date. I discovered something of importance in my life, or, rather, the only important thing that has ever happened to me. It was the account I made of a part of my life. A batch of written tales set aside for a doctor who'd prescribed them. Reading and rereading these, I find it easy to put things in the places where they belong, places my inexperience had prevented me from finding. How alive that life is, and how definitively dead the part I didn't recount. I look for it sometimes, anxiously, feeling amputated, but it's nowhere to be found. I know, too, that the part I told was not the most important part. It became the most important because I obsessed about it. And now what have I become? Not a man who lived, but a man who wrote things down. Ah! The only thing that matters in life is collecting one's thoughts. When everybody else understands this as clearly as I do, they will all write. Life will be literaturized. Half of humanity will devote itself to reading and studying what the other half has put down. And contemplation will take up as much time as possible—time to be subtracted from horrid real life. If one part of humanity rebels and refuses to read the lucubrations of the other part, so much the better. Each person will read himself. And whether each life becomes clearer or murkier, it will evolve, correct, crystallize. At least it won't remain what it is, undistinguished, buried as soon as it's birthed, with those days that fade away and accumulate, one identical to the next, to form years, decades, a life so empty it merely serves as a number in a statistical table of demographic trends. I want to start writing again. I'll put my whole self and my every incident in these pages. They call me a grumbler at home. I'll surprise them. I won't open my mouth, and grumble only on the page. I'm not made to fight, and so when they suggest that I'm no longer able to understand things, rather than deny it or try to prove I can still look after myself and my family, I'll run here to regain my peace of mind . . .

I'll discover that the person written about here is quite different from the one I recorded years ago. Life, even when not written down, leaves its mark. I think one grows more serene with time. I no longer suffer that foolish remorse, those terrifying fears of the future. How could it terrorize me? I'm living that future now. And it spins by without creating another. So this is not even a real present, it's out of time. There's no ultimate tense in my grammar. Yes, I did think the rejuvenation procedure would change things. However, I decided upon it capriciously, and was always ambivalent, confused, forever about to change my mind, with one ear out in case my wife, my daughter, or my son began to insist that I should stop. But no one did, most likely they wanted to witness that amazing operation, which in any case would cost them nothing. And so I went along, suffering and concealing it. First I compromised myself with my wife and my daughter, broadcasting my intentions in an attempt to frighten and punish them; and then on the telephone with the doctor, once again hoping to frighten and punish him, and so I ended up on the operating table entirely against my will. Afterwards came a case of boils that has confined me to my bedroom for a month.

All the same, old age is the peaceful stage of life. So peaceful it's not easy to record. Where to grab hold, to begin to describe what led up to the surgery? The aftermath is easy. The expectation of the youthfulness the operation was meant to bring was itself a kind of youthfulness, a period of hard suffering and great hopes. I see how my life began in infancy, passed through a turbulent adolescence that one day subsided into youth—a sort of disenchantment—and then plunged into marriage, resignation interrupted by the occasional rebellion, and from there to old age, the main thrust of which has been to cast me in shadow and eliminate my role as protagonist. For everyone, even for me, my life served to enhance the importance of the others—my wife, my daughter, my son, and my grandson. Then came the operation, and everyone looked on me with admiration. I grew excited, returned to an earlier stage of life quite like what my own had been—I mean the life that doesn't require operations, natural life, the one everyone has—and excitement led me to these pages, which I think I should never have abandoned. Justified though my self-reproof is, it's not more convincing than the shame of that other old man who felt he had withered because he no longer had women. I'm writing because I must, when once a pen in hand would have made me yawn. I think the operation has had a salutary effect.

I

And so I must begin where I left off. The war had ended in the fashion everyone knows, and to the general victory I planned to add my own particular victory: I intended to show old Olivi how successful I'd been at managing my affairs without him. But the old man, who had never paid me the least notice, went and died of the flu in Pisa so as not to have to admire me—after he'd already informed me when he would be arriving and I had written to say what his duties would henceforth be. That is, he'd be running the office, while I would be managing the business. I awaited him impatiently; if he'd gotten there in time he might have spared me a serious loss, the purchase of all those railcars of soap sitting in Milan, waiting for the frontiers to open to make a colossal killing. The prospect of such a deal stirred my wartime instincts, while Olivi had another type of experience that might, once the armistice was signed, have been useful. I bought a gigantic portion of stock and was in no hurry to sell, as one isn't, in war. Was there a widespread need to wash? You only had to board the tram in Trieste to notice an intense stink—to me, a heavenly smell that reassured me about the soap operation. When I learned of Olivi's death I was somewhat irked: he had escaped his downfall! Later,

I was glad, for nobody in Trieste was interested in my soap. Did they no longer wash? It would have been a sorry day had Olivi come to find that most of the profits of war had been consumed in a deal made in peacetime. I was all alone liquidating that business. And I didn't reproach myself at all. The world had evolved so quickly that I had slipped off and was sailing unknown seas. That soap I bought in Milan didn't have the fat content prescribed by the Austrian law that still governed Trieste despite the presence of Italian troops. So I sold the soap on three-month credit to an Austrian, who then departed for Vienna where it was to be shipped. There, either because it was urgently needed or because it didn't meet legal standards, the soap was confiscated. The bureau that took charge of it eventually paid full price. But the kronen only got here when it was too late to exchange them and were finally worth only a few lire.

That was my last deal, and I still recall it from time to time. One never forgets one's first deal, spoiled by one's naiveté, or the last, a catastrophe because one's overly shrewd. And I haven't forgotten mine because there's a certain amount of rancor involved. Just before I liquidated the shipment, young Olivi came back from the war. The bespectacled young lieutenant's chest was adorned with medals. He agreed to take up his old duties under my direction. And I quickly got used to the very comfortable role of a ruler who doesn't govern. Very soon, I knew nothing of my own business. Every day new Italian laws and decrees poured down, written in an incomprehensible language of which the only thing certain was the numeral that designated our king. I let Olivi deal with all the documents and the tax stamps (it was then that the nation began to wet countless stamps). When the man became quite disagreeable, I avoided the office. He was always talking about his merits and his hardships during the war, never missing a chance to reproach me for not having played my part in the victory.

Speaking of soap and the now worthless kronen, I once said to him, "But there must be some way we can go after the Viennese. We won the war, didn't we?" He laughed in my face. I'm convinced that just to prove I hadn't won the war, he never did anything to force the Austrians to compensate me.

Otherwise, he devoted himself to my business with great diligence. He was devoted, too, to my son Alfio, who, after he dropped out of the gymnasium, would come to the office from time to time to gain experience. Then he quit, when he took up painting—but it was clear Olivi didn't mind some supervision.

Nor did he mind being supervised by my son-in-law Valentino. Now there was a worker! All day long pursuing business, and every night more than an hour going over Olivi's books. Then, alas, he fell ill and died, but thanks to his efforts I place the same trust in the young Olivi that my father and I had in the elder. Indeed, one might say more, because old Olivi was never supervised very carefully at any time in his life. My father knew nothing of accounting, I suspect, while I went into the office from time to time, but mostly to deal with my own affairs rather than supervise someone else. Anyway, I've never been good at the books. I can do business—that is, dream up and carry out a deal—but when I'm finished it all becomes a fog and I don't know how to record it. I think this must be the case with all real businessmen, otherwise when one operation is done they wouldn't be able to conceive another. In any case, I stopped going to the office. But I'm ready and waiting. If another war comes along I'll go back to work.

Now that I've mentioned him, let me say something about Alfio. It will be good to collect my thoughts, because I really don't know how to handle him. He came back home after the war, a big lad of fifteen—quite a bit different from the boy who left—tall and gangly now and carelessly dressed. I could see right off he was easily distracted, incapable of continuing today what he'd begun the day before— qualities, in short, that I was quite familiar with and that the great cyclone had cured me of. I believed I would take care not to repeat my father's mistakes, that I'd be capable of treating my son differently. My God, though! Woe to my poor father, had he been dealt such a son. I was far better prepared than he by my culture and my experience to endure such novelties, and yet even I couldn't think how to look at him, tolerate him. I let him do whatever he wanted. He dropped out of gymnasium right after the Gentile Reform, which didn't suit him, and I didn't utter a single word of protest. I merely pointed out that he was forfeiting his chance of academic standing; I must have been somewhat upset because I too was sacrificing hopes. He felt mine was an intolerable interference, and told me that what stood between us was not just a difference in age but much, much more. The war stood between us. We were now living in a new world I didn't belong to because I was born before the war. But I thought I understood everything in this world quite well, and found it infuriating to be treated as an imbecile.

In truth, our dispute was fomented by others. It exploded one Sunday after the midday meal. We'd dined with my wife, my daughter Antonia, Valentino, and Carlo, Ada and Guido's son who was studying medicine in Bologna and was staying with us for the holidays. Carlo started trying to persuade Alfio not to abandon his education, on the simple grounds that while gymnasium was fairly oppressive, he'd find university far more agreeable. "One studies," said Carlo, "almost without being aware of it." I was pretty much in a foul humor. I find the vegetarian diet Dr. Raulli has imposed on me harder on a Sunday, when I must sit and watch everyone around me devouring choice poultry meat. And yet I'm sure I didn't complicate the discussion by speaking of sacrifice in a bitter tone. I was the mildest one of all. It simply wasn't possible to discourage all those allies who wanted to urge Alfio in the direction that I too favored and in which I alone was unable to force him. Valentino—he had the soul of a bureaucrat, confident that all things in this world can be easily explained, and that you merely need to arrive at a precise count to have the explanation—took an aggressive approach. He argued that everyone must learn to sacrifice, for his future, for his own dignity, for his own family. That was just how it was. Anyone who couldn't adjust to such a rule would regret it. He knew this because he had often seen it. He couldn't speak from his own experience, because he'd understood the principle right from the beginning and had begun in early youth to do everything that was necessary to guarantee his future.

Carlo mocked Valentino a little. "You'll find there are people in this world who prefer the present to always thinking about the future.

They're simply two verb tenses, of equal merit grammatically. We're all free to prefer one or the other."

He was only teasing, but his comment poisoned the discussion, I think. Alfio didn't want to side with Carlo, from whom he was very different, and tried to distance himself further, but ended up colliding with Valentino. "It's not true that everyone in this world can understand everything. A clerk, for example, can't understand an artist. And neither can a doctor."

Carlo had inherited many defects from his father, Guido, but not the lack of wit that ruined him (the man was capable of holding the most ridiculous opinions without being able to laugh at them), and now he made a show of indifference, taking a sip from his glass. "It's true, we doctors understand nothing of artists beyond the fits that afflict them from time to time. In such cases they're no longer artists and finally stop getting on other people's nerves."

Valentino was silent. He was something of a weakling. He'd recently begun to review the firm's books, for my benefit he thought, and genuinely believed he'd been charged with protecting the good fortune of the entire family. He'd been mistaken in what he said about sacrifice, and was amply ready to change his mind. He merely launched a timid protest in Alfio's direction: "I can only offer the advice suggested by my experience."

But Antonia was ferocious. She usually treats Alfio somewhat maternally, but now she saw her husband under attack. She thought Carlo's levity in speaking of Valentino's very serious considerations showed his special contempt for her husband. She became violent; she blamed me for giving my boy too much freedom to commit serious errors (here I raised my two arms as if to invoke God's assistance) and scolded Alfio for thinking he was superior to the others. Sooner or later he'd have to repent of that arrogance. Why would he not at least finish middle school? He'd be inferior to everybody all his life. And moreover, when someone was inclined to offer good advice he shouldn't reply so rudely.

The result of this argument, which involved me not at all, was that Alfio developed a deep grudge against me. It's true that I didn't support him, or rather that I wasn't able to refrain from siding with the others. My God! It's dreadful to see your son step off, right at the start, the road taken by everybody capable of taking it. I couldn't, however, risk criticizing Valentino and causing more pain to Antonia. Many years ago I vowed not to reproduce between my son and myself the relations I had with my father, and here I was, on the brink of doing just that. I had tried to make sure that there were no excessive displays of feeling between us, nothing like that painful anxiety which my father, as he lay dying, expressed for my future. At that moment, when he was already suffering terribly, his concern was like a passionate kiss that surely must have provoked my own lengthy, painful condition, an ailment that, even after I was well again, made me see the sun as dimmed and feel the air as heavy.

To this end, I intended to avoid great shows of affection between myself and my son, and also shied away from playing the patriarch. Those shows of affection weren't difficult to banish when the boy was a baby, not least because I've never been able to tolerate the indecorous screams of little children. As far as playing the patriarch went, I couldn't completely avoid it. When Augusta lost all patience, she'd call for my help and I would step in with a great shout that put paid to all arguments. But this was brief and usually directed at both the boy and his sister indiscriminately, the way a general reprimands an entire army corps—and then quickly annulled by me with some teasing words that made it clear I bore no grudges. I never asked them to make any acts of contrition. I believe I succeeded with Antonia: she'll be able to experience my death with great serenity and continue life alongside her husband and her son as if I'd never lived. She'll happily come to put flowers on my tomb each year, convinced she's giving me all the pleasure I'm entitled to.

But I'm less sure about Alfio. He doesn't hold me in great esteem, I know. For an artist like Alfio, a businessman is a creature unworthy of notice. It is just this kind of judgment that death can rectify. And yet, while it should have been quite simple to have unclouded relations with my father, with whom I lived alone and with whom any complications could only derive from him or me, here there is a whole crowd of people obscuring our relations. To give just one example, let's return to the argument of that Sunday. At one point I raised my arms in a gesture that is, more than any other, patriarchal, and I did so to calm Antonia down. Yet I was unable to allow my son to make his own decisions and intervened with a rebuke, which I rationalized as a sign of my affection, when in fact I was reacting to Valentino.

In short, young Alfio is far more difficult for me to handle than I was for my father. My father reproached me for laughing at everything, and my son reproaches me for the same. Apart from the distress that such a thing provokes in me, my son's stance is far more rigid than my father's was: in effect he made me laugh, while my son is tougher, more forceful. I try to be serious, and when something crazy pops into my head, I do my best to drive it out. When it's gone, I look back at it with regret. Unspoken, it dwindles to nothing, and life goes on more monotonous and drearier than ever.

To tell the truth, I believe my son bears me a grudge, and his mother too. At the slightest disagreement, there's always a squeal of resentment in his voice, which is rather weak anyway. Just after the war, the grudge had to do with communism. He wasn't really a communist, but he genuinely considered us scoundrels because we took up a lot of space (owned a house with many rooms) and because so much of our property was private, when it would have been useful to everyone. Augusta was terrified that he'd come home one day with new tenants. But he didn't know a single worker in this world. He walked the streets alone, busy thinking about social justice one minute, and the next, at the same pace, about art, about *personality*. And that was when I laughed at him a bit, but I was wrong. His concerns were still theoretical; he hadn't yet taken up painting. I felt this business of personality was excessive, presumptuous. One must be a lovable type, a seductive personality, that was the idea. But what was this personality? Real personalities were people who could end up in prison for life. "What a personality," I would say of our Giacomo, the night watchman we'd recently hired so that our villa would be better guarded in these uncertain times. Giacomo was a real personality. When he was loaded with wine he was savage like a drunk, but unable to play the part: he just seemed savage, not drunk. He didn't stumble, and walked the same straight line as when he was sober, only a little stiffly. I never sent him away. He did his duty, always on the alert. Anyway he never had to do anything, and we always slept well because nothing special ever happened. A personality.

But Alfio got angry and, as usual, in explaining himself insulted me. I became a bit savage myself and threatened to disinherit him. The dispute went on for many days, with Augusta running from one to the other to clarify, soften, negotiate. My own rage was now burnt out, but Alfio, to please his mother, ended up asking my forgiveness, but then he never forgave me again. In truth I was always very busy and wouldn't have given the matter much thought, but I didn't like to see him so moody when we met. I was conscious that death hovered near me, and I was sorry for Alfio, who would have to endure the same troubles that clouded my own youth. And I felt sorry for myself too: seeing me dead, my only son would probably heave a sigh of relief and say "Phew!" Alfio's sincerity was of the radical sort: the right word was important. Whereas I preferred to die and be mourned, with the appropriate moderation of course.

From Augusta I learned that Alfio was a solitary painter. He'd go out in the morning with his map under his arm and his tempera paints, taking along something to eat. He didn't have anyone instructing him, lest a teacher would cut down his personality. When the sun set he'd come home dead tired. Nevertheless, he'd go out again to the caffè to talk painting with his friends. This part of the day was the only thing he'd inherited from me. The rest of it wasn't mine, nor his grandfather's, nor his grandmother's either. Where had he turned up those paintings and that solitude of his? Personality? I, who had always sought—in vain—to look like everybody else, had never given it a thought. Rebellion? When I felt that desire I repented instantly. His grandfather Giovanni had no idea what rebellion was, he was large and fat and sat so comfortably on the backs of others. When rebellion is congenital, as it was with Alfio, it's a real mark of weakness.

He'd even invented his own body type; none of his ancestors had anything like it. Tall, spindly, a curious set of the trunk tending to retrocede, then reversing again higher up, forming rounded shoulders that aren't, however, a hunchback, his head tilted forward, so that he never stood completely erect and his eyes are forced to turn upward to look into the face of an interlocutor of his own height. He's not handsome: I know that because other people tell me so. But Augusta and I admire his white, sweet face. It's of course quite another thing to know a person intimately, rather than just see him pass by once, his imperfections evident. We knew what Alfio's strengths and weaknesses were. His long legs were more than just shapely. And Augusta and I often spoke of the magnificent expression of Alfio's intensely blue eyes, one of which was slightly askew, but not as much as one of his mother's: bright blue eyes that demanded help and support, poor things, off kilter and having to make an effort to see, while from his mouth came ugly words from the writings of Marx—writings he'd never read and didn't believe in.

I felt I must make my peace with him. One day I was feeling worse than usual: an apoplexy seemed to lie in wait, one of those terrible ordeals that steals your speech, your hearing, your sight, when it doesn't take your life. It announced itself with a certain buzzing in the ears. One time they measured my blood pressure at 230 mm! And I was moved to think of poor Alfio standing by my corpse, murmuring as I did in my day, "Well, that's it, my life is finished."

I went to see him in the evening as soon as I knew he'd returned home and was dressing to go out to the caffè. He had a studio on the other side of the house, not very bright but charmingly arranged by Augusta.

"May I?" I asked a little hesitantly, the door halfway open. I saw Alfio in front of the mirror knotting his necktie, gazing up at himself. It's a sign of real sincerity when a person looks at himself the same way he looks at other people.

He turned to me, tie gracing a shirt that was none too fresh. He seemed quite surprised and was very concerned. "You came all this way, Papa? Why didn't you call for me?"

Relieved, I began to laugh. "It's business, and better that we should discuss it alone. I know from what your mother tells me that you finish a painting every day. Couldn't I have one?"

He looked at me, doubtful, diffident, although his eye was pleading. "But Father! It isn't art for everyone. It's a new art, and one must comprehend it. Because it's new, it's quite rough; a collection of signs nearly ungoverned by impressions."

"Why argue?" I laughed. "Old art, new art, it can all be bought. You paint it in order to sell it. Sell me one of your works. I'll be your first client."

He seemed to be about to protest, but after thinking about it briefly he agreed. He then bashfully mentioned something that might have been a sum.

"How much?" I asked, a little too loudly.

He stared at me hesitantly, red to his ears. You see, he thought I wanted to argue about the sum he'd named. I got a real scare. What if he lowered his price to please me, and that led him to feel the sort of rancor felt by people who've been forced to reduce their prices? How conciliatory would that be?

I began to plead with him. "Look, I'm old and I don't hear well. Tell me how much you want. I'll pay whatever you ask in order to know you and your art better. I'll hang your work on my study wall and I'll look at it every day. And in the end, I too will understand it. I'm less of a cretin than you think. I'm old, that's true. But as a result I have some experience. It's true that I never studied painting, but music, yes. I've even come to be able to tolerate Debussy recently. Love him, no. To me his things sound like they've recently been exploded by a bomb. The fragments are still smoking, although there's nothing else linking them together."

I think Alfio decided to please me after I rambled on about Debussy.

He stated his price, resolute. Eight hundred lire.

I drew a thousand-lire bill from my pocket and, speaking like a proper businessman, said, "You owe me two hundred lire." Then, pretending I was impatient: "So, where is the painting?"

He gave me the two hundred. He's very correct with money, despite his completely unseemly ideas about wealth. He's quite superior to me in this regard, and that superiority of his, much admired by his mother, pleases me. He never spends anything, and therefore is like his impoverished friends, but his wallet is always full, so in that way he is different.

As for the painting, he still hadn't given it to me. He'd bring it along in ten minutes. He wanted to choose his best work. Modesty, it seemed, prevented him from showing me his early experiments.

I began to walk toward the door, then turned back to him. "You know," I began, "we two are alone in this world." Then I stopped, frightened of having said the same thing as my father once had, far more truthfully. I corrected myself. "What I mean is that we are the only two men related by blood in this household. Why don't we understand one another? I mean to make every effort to know you better. Will you do the same? I can no longer teach you anything and I don't want to behave like a schoolmaster. I'm too old to teach and you're too old to learn. You have your own personality, my son, and you must do your best to realize it."

I kissed his cheek, and he, confused, kissed the air. "Yes, Papa," he said. He was moved.

I cheerfully made for the door. "Bring nails to hang your picture right away. You know I don't know how to do such things."

"But a painting must have a frame," he told me. "I'll buy one tomorrow. A small, modest frame for a small, modest picture."

"That's fine," I said, "but meanwhile I want to begin to study your painting right away. You'll know how to hang it without damaging it."

While I waited for Alfio those ten minutes, I was keyed up. I had done a great thing, I felt, for me, for him, for the family. My father wouldn't have been able to do the same. And there hadn't been any Great War between him and me. War? You just needed intelligence to connect with the other generation. The thought of war returned, however, when I saw the square of paper with the picture on it. I was looking over Alfio's shoulder while he was busy nailing it to the wall.

"Thank you, thank you," I said. He stood admiring it for an instant.

And I did the same. Then, with that slightly flabby gait, he left the room.

When I looked at his painting again, I thought, "He's cheated me; he's given me his worst painting." It's by no means unpleasant to discover that your son has a talent for business. I made my peace with it.

From the beginning it was distasteful to have that ugly thing before my eyes. Before I saw it I'd asked Alfio to hang it where I could see it while I was sitting at my desk. And Alfio did an excellent job. I could see it not only from the desk, but also when I sat reading with the lamp behind my back, and even when I stretched out on the sofa to rest. Unless, that is, I rested on my left side—something I can't bear, just as my father couldn't bear it—with my nose to the wall. And even then I felt the presence of that little horror in the room.

That painting convinced me that within my family (my father, my son, and me) my levelheaded self-possession was the great exception.

There was no way to remove the picture without the risk of reviving Alfio's contempt. The frame arrived and then the painting was returned to its place, although I'd timidly suggested moving it to take advantage of better light. Alfio, sounding very sure of himself, explained that no, the picture belonged in just that spot. He looked at it once more, admiring the splendid isolation the frame provided, and went out.

The frame was like a comment; anything that's enclosed in a frame takes on value, I suppose. A thing must be isolated in order to become something. Otherwise it's obfuscated by what's nearby. Alfio's painting would become something. I studied it, first irked, then more compassionately, as I began to understand what he'd intended, and finally admiringly, when I suddenly discovered he really had painted something.

To begin with, it was clear that Alfio had wanted to paint a hill. There was no doubt of it. The colors didn't vary, no matter how far in the distance or how high up, but when I came to understand and love that painting I saw things that changed how the air around me looked. Three parallel rows of houses had been built, or were supposed to have been built, on the hill. Studying these, I felt pleasantly like I was collaborating with Alfio. I was painting too. Below, the street was marked by a few brushstrokes of purple. It wasn't the usual color of ground. But still, it was easy to see it must be ground. Above stood the first row of buildings: a long yellow wall and in one corner a single house, also yellow at the top, and underneath plain white, the color of the paper. This house, though, was the most habitable of all. The walls, truly perpendicular, were perfectly built, and the only defect was the scarcity of windows, two on the second floor and one on the first, but all of them fitted with proper shutters painted a gray that, later, I would love. This was surely the manor house. Beyond this first row there were other dabs of that purplish color that as the key within the painting made clear, marked another road. Then there were two other rows of houses divided by the same purple, bolder here because of the distance, so that they could be seen better. But what houses, my God! All a poet's compassion for poor derelict homes was in them, like a discreet lament. Most of the walls stood at right angles, but there were no windows, or where there were, they were decidedly black and shapeless enough to suggest they had no shutters or even glass. Rather than reflect the light outside, they let the dismal gloom that was inside seep out.

It's quite amazing how one can accustom oneself to anything in this world. I loved that painting, and when I raised my face from my book (I'd begun to read philosophy again and was studying Nietzsche) I really enjoyed finding myself in front of that portrait of life as Alfio saw it. I peopled those houses. In the manor house, I put some masters as vulgar as their dwellings, who exploited the people in the black-windowed houses. High up in the painting, in the distance, there was another house, well built and true, although its windows were black—and this resembled a second manor house. It seemed to me that if there were two masters' houses, the other houses were even worse off. Poor meek, tumbledown houses of suffering. There were also some dabs that suggested that the houses of the destitute could still multiply. Some abandoned turrets that looked like with time they could be converted to habitations.

This was a very pleasant period in my relations with Alfio. I sincerely admired him. By painting the shutters on a single house, he'd given me leave to create an entire landscape. His was true art. A modern sort of art, and in making sense of it, I was growing younger.

I was deeply satisfied and I told Alfio so. He listened. But with his typical youthful energy he interrupted me, and my praise was squandered. The ground, viewed from a particular spot at that particular time of day, really was that color. It didn't require courage to invent it but the painter's analytic eye to see it. "Look, you must look carefully," he said.

Wanting to resume my analysis, I began to talk about the houses that weren't yet there, but which one could see forming.

He laughed, protesting. "But those are houses, you merely have to look to see they're real. You must know how to look. Remember, the light doesn't always reveal, sometimes it obfuscates, it hides. Look at that house you think isn't there yet: there's a faint brown mark suggesting a window."

It was easier, I felt, to endure the painting than his comments. I continued to look at it happily, but when we spoke of it I used Alfio's words and didn't bother to say what I thought. I was sure, though, that if I had turned up in that landscape I could have found my way around with no fear of getting lost. The agreeable period of my relations with Alfio went on for a long time, only slightly disturbed by Alfio's gift of a second painting that I didn't want to hang on my study wall. I put it in a drawer, assuring my son that I looked at it every day. It wasn't true: I didn't have time to people all his ramshackle houses. And there wasn't much room to use my imagination, because I couldn't say what I thought but had to repeat Alfio's words. It was easier not to look at his paintings.

This happy time ended abruptly. In a moment of great joy, and just when I wasn't expecting it. I'd invited an old friend to luncheon, a man named Orazio Cima whom I hadn't seen for nearly half a century. In old age, meetings like this resemble words printed in italics in a book: they have a special significance. I hadn't forgotten Cima for several reasons. He was a landowner with huge properties in the south, who had come to Trieste to study German as a young man. The young man quickly learned to speak not German, but the Triestine dialect; in those days southerners made these mistakes. He spent his days courting women and going hunting and fishing. He was wealthier in those days than he would ever be again.

I couldn't have forgotten him, because he stood for various of my failures in life, as well as one of my successes. And in judging my life I intend to be sternly objective, so I had forgotten neither the one nor the other.

My success was one of observation. In those days I was studying political economy. That is, I was studying law at the time, but in my diligence I was deeply immersed in political economy, meant to be only a secondary subject.

Now Cima was evidently an absentee *latifondista*, a figure very thoroughly described in my textbooks. One day while he was in my presence, Orazio received a letter from his factor. "It's from the factor," he murmured. Even today, an old man, he mutters the words he's thinking, doubtless to exercise his brain, which is precise but slow. When he had read the letter, he murmured, "No." And I said, "I'll bet your factor proposed some improvements that you refused." "How did you know?" he said, surprised. And I was able to name the textbook I'd learned it from.

The failures were many, and obviously I don't remember them all. One time I persuaded him to stop smoking with me. Of course I gave in and smoked again right away. He instead was able to tolerate all the hunting adventures, both good and bad, that came his way in a week, without ever going back on his vow. One day he tramped over the Carso for ten hours without bagging a single animal; the next, he shot so many that he had to return to the city early, or his prize load would have been too heavy. His resolution was constant throughout. It was quite surprising to me; I'm unable to quit smoking because my determination collapses when the news is good, when it's bad, and when there's no news at all.

The force of his will was like inertia, like a state of being, like the water's determination to rush down the mountain. When faced with someone else's wishes, if they did not coincide with his own, he behaved as if he were deaf. Once—I remember it as if it were yesterday, because one doesn't forget great indignation—I was expected by a lady who had reserved an hour, no more, for me at six. At three I foolishly boarded a trap he was driving, and he took me all the way to Lipizza. It was a beautiful, crisp fall day, but I recall it as a dark one, steeped in rage.

At a certain hour, we might still have returned to Trieste in time, but in spite of my urging he took me on a tour of the Carso, with which I'm so unfamiliar that I thought we were on the road to the city. When we did get to Trieste, I stood in the middle of the square where he had dumped me, twisted with desire and regret. Orazio, all innocence, said, "But you should have informed me before we left." Of course I had told him, but it was one of those things he was deaf to. He undertook this annoying journey, I later learned, because his veterinarian had advised him that his horse needed to trot a certain number of kilometers a day.

Now that he had returned to Trieste, he assured me glumly that he had lived so long and suffered so much that he no longer felt desire. For my part, I assured him I was no longer the weak-willed fellow he once knew. I found it hard to believe him, because I felt as if I'd returned to Lipizza with him that very day, but doing a stiff trot myself, rather than being pulled by the horse. He wanted me to come with him here, there, and everywhere. "I'll take you home now," he said, as we stopped at an insurance company where he needed to sign a declaration that he'd changed domicile for a moving company that still had some of his furniture in its warehouse. And then he inflicted old Ducci on me.

Old Ducci, like me, had never left Trieste, but since the day we left school at eighteen we had never exchanged a word. I remember that the last time we spoke, he'd told me he wanted to go and seek his fortune in Japan. After that we saw each other nearly every week—our city is small—and nodded greetings to one another without ever speaking. As the years went by, our greetings became ever more cordial. The fact that we were the only ones in town to have known each other so long created a certain intimacy. I found it natural that he had foregone Japan once he made his fortune in Trieste. And now here we were, the three of us, on a sidewalk weighed down by nearly two centuries of life. We gazed at each other in a friendly way, eyes going glassy with age, and for a moment I forgot my impatience. It returned only when I learned that Ducci didn't remember ever having had the intention to go to Japan. Good God! My whole world shook. For so many years, every time I ran into the fellow, I thought, "There he is, the man who almost went to Japan." Had I been mistaken, had someone else, those fifty years ago, told me he wanted to emigrate? Then, having seen Ducci a number of times during Cima's stay in Trieste, I discovered that he was a man of great projects. For instance, he was longing to go to Norway. Certainly it was possible that in the making of his many plans in the upcoming fifty years, he might forget about Norway too, while I, who avoid plans because they make me uneasy, might—if I live that long—remember his very astounding one.

The first time Cima came to luncheon, he told an old story from our youth that he only knew part of, and which I then completed, and we actually got so drunk laughing that in our jolly abandon I offended my poor Alfio quite irreparably.

You should know that when the younger Cima first came to Trieste, I was studying those around me in search of models of strength and resolution who could cure me of the weakness I'd begun to be so afflicted by. What better model than Cima? That masterly air he always had, and the fact that he was unacquainted with doubts or embarrassment, albeit much less intelligent than I: these could benefit me. He looked very strong and youthful, with his diminutive Spanish beard, black eyes, and thick, curly hair. I couldn't imitate his good looks and his strength, but I didn't believe that they were responsible for the influence he exerted, from which he drew great peace of mind, certainty, and happiness. He was the master because he knew he was.

And it seemed to me that his habit of killing animals had helped to build Cima's strength. This was my true weakness—the worst—being unable to kill animals. My revulsion was such—and I remember it well because even today, I experience something similar, if less intense—that one evening, just before getting into bed, I landed a light blow on a fly that was tormenting me. The creature, wounded, managed to escape; in my compassion, I tried to recapture it and finish it off, but in vain. I couldn't find it, and during the night I thought many times about that poor rancorous, suffering beast, agonizing in some hidden corner of the room. And so I decided, with Cima as my guide, to learn to live with such remorse. I paid a stiff tax for hunting privileges and purchased a smart hunter's costume with a feathered hat, like we used to wear. Cima lent me the shotgun.

We began with swamp hunting. Our destination was some wetlands near Cervignano. On the way there I tried to fill my heart with hatred for my prey. Those birds I was going to shoot were predators themselves. They lived on smaller birds. It was said that when they were dealing with a dangerous animal of some sort, they had no qualms about taking it in their beak, flying high and letting it fall, killing it. I learned that even if I shot game I was still superior to Cima, who, like a proper hunting dog, didn't even like game, while I could drown my remorse with a nice meal. In any case I was very agitated, and this first violent foray against animals seemed so important to me that I smoked a great number of cigarettes, telling myself that once I had acquired a strong will—an assassin's will—I would stop smoking.

I was meaning to tell of recent events, tales of just a few weeks ago, but here I find myself in the distant past. Old things come to seem very important compared with those of just a few weeks ago. It's like the smell of old wine, composed of an array of elements that light up one's memory as they approach the nose. There's my wife, who claims I remember nothing. Certainly if I am asked where I left my gold pen and spectacles, I'm taken aback to have to make such an effort. But old things come to me all by themselves, numerous and adorned with all their details.

So there we were in the swamp, each of us hidden in a barrel sunk in the mud, a certain distance apart. Orazio advised me to stay calm and show no signs of life, because we would have to endure many hours in the wet of our barrels to fool those suspicious birds, animals that scrutinize the path they intend to take at length with their tiny, powerful eyes before showing themselves. All that caution, a further reason to despise them! Above the distant mountains, the sky seemed to be growing lighter. Was this the dawn? I was getting very nervous. Things that move slowly make me impatient. How could I speed this up, this having to stand there on my feet in such an uncomfortable place? Damn Cima! He could have arranged for me to have a larger barrel, and put a chair in it at least. I tried to look at my watch. It was one way to make time move faster. But all the light from those quiet stars observing me, that gigantic model of patience, was not enough to illuminate the little dial. An idea came to me: I could stop smoking at an unidentified time. It was a completely new kind of resolution, which would be more difficult to break. No more calculations, no more counting days. I would start at an unidentified point to arrive at another, distant unidentified point.

I investigated which side of the barrel the wind was coming from, and leaned against that side. Carefully, I lit a match.

And then something outrageous happened. Cima fired his gun at me. I could hear the buckshot whistling past my ears. And I was thoroughly indignant. In those days I was thoroughly indignant at anyone who tried to prevent me from having my last cigarette. So you can imagine how I felt about something like this. I didn't give it a minute's thought. Cima was hurling insults at me, but instead of replying I shouted, "I'm going to kill you," pointed the shotgun at him, and fired.

"Idiot," shouted Cima. "What do you think you're doing?"

"What do you think *you're* doing?" said I.

"But I know how to shoot."

"If I hadn't ducked my head I'd have buckshot in my eye."

"And I have a hole in my hat," as he jumped out of the barrel and brought it over for me to see.

I was sorry. I could have said that I'd aimed at his hat and not his head, but he wouldn't have believed me.

"I'm sorry," I said, "but you made me very angry." He cast a regretful eye over the vast swampland and turned to go.

"No, you stay," I said, my face set, smoking furiously. "I'm going."

"To do what?" he said, lighting a cigarette. "By this time all the birds around know we have guns here. Anyway, you'll never find your way out of the swamp alone. Look at you: mud up to your knees." He turned his back on me and strode off.

It was his way of obliging me to follow, but I didn't want to take orders from him. Although drowning was a real danger. I fought my way out of the mud and got up on the path he'd taken. There was nothing to do but resign myself and submit, for the last time. I made a vow: In the future, whenever he went to Boschetto, I would go to Servola. At Servola, one was dealing with solid ground. "What a funny fellow you are!" He was laughing so hard he almost fell over, and just managed to get out a few broken phrases: "I fire . . . you fire . . . as if it was the same thing." He lit a match. "And now it's you who's angry with me!" He grabbed my arm, patting it. And I ended up laughing with him. It would have been silly to stop smoking at an unidentified time.

A good laugh, now there's something that doesn't wear out. Especially when we reencounter it just as it was, and even heartier. In that gaunt old man—a modest figure who always stood quite erect, not out of natural vigor but because feeble and frail as he was, no strength whatsoever was needed to keep him upright, and someone jostling could have inadvertently knocked him over; with his head still partly covered with white hair (a lot more than I had, but not enough to disguise the blushing pink skin underneath)—I found my old friend, now gentler, less dangerous. He was no longer as tireless as he'd been when he was a model and a teacher, certainly; he was more like a teacher who has nothing more to teach, who's content to be treated on equal terms. We laughed about my stupidity in wanting to go hunting, and his for having taken me. And then we laughed about my stupidity alone, because Augusta started talking about my long-standing struggle to swear off cigarettes. They ended up agreeing that, to my credit, my disease must be cured, because I never mentioned it, though I still smoked. How about that! I'd even forced my disease never to show itself, except in monologues soon forgotten and resolutions left unwritten, unspoken, and unmarked on any calendar or watch face, which left me in a rather enjoyable state of freedom. Damn it! Long life cures all ailments.

Now, I had nothing to drink at that luncheon, and I even abstained from the fine roast that everyone else was eating. Nothing at all, in other words, went into my poor blood to heat it up. Sheer laughing made it boil. I laughed at myself, who had set out to kill animals and was such a good shot that not a single grain of buckshot struck poor Cima. Then, to provoke him, I corrected myself: I had gone out to shoot animals, and animals had ended up shooting at me. And Cima also came up with something, which I don't recall, but at which everyone laughed except me. It was a poor joke, I'd have had to tickle myself in order to laugh. But there were no hard feelings between us. Although naturally that was the end of the laughing, while I'd have liked to continue. It's a healthy discipline, and the only violent one the old are permitted.

To prolong the moment I began to talk about Alfio's painting, something I had laughed about in the past, though somewhat sourly, and that I smiled about now, thinking of my efforts to find things in it that weren't there, and how I had ended up fond of it even as I went on laughing. There had been much talk of earthquakes in those days, and I was nearly exploding with laughter as I explained how I had run to look at Alfio's painting to see whether the tiny, miserable houses in it had collapsed. "No, they hadn't. They looked like they had fallen down, but they stood exactly as they had before."

Even the sight of Alfio's white face as it suddenly blanched even whiter didn't hold me back. My attack had been so unexpected that he raised his head slightly from his plate and trained his sweet eyes on my face to determine whether there might be another intention beneath my apparent derision. I noticed nothing. I felt quite innocent: I just wanted to laugh, and any topic would do.

Alfio burst out, "Look, if you want I'll return the money you paid me, and take my work back."

But I retorted, "And who's going to pay me for the work *I* put into it?"

And seeing that slow-minded Cima didn't understand what I was talking about, I explained that with some effort and persistence I had managed to fill out and populate the houses in my son's picture, and now that I had done so I didn't wish to give them back. Now that the painting was finished, I quite liked it. And just as soon as I was back in full possession of my health (for a month now I've been taking a tonic to that effect), I would dedicate myself to another painting that I was keeping hidden away to avoid being forced to make such an effort again.

Alfio tried to attack. "You know, what costs you an effort, others, better prepared to appreciate art, can do effortlessly, just by looking, the way one simply looks at nature."

Now I got angry and denied that I had to make an effort because of my deficiencies. I grew so angry that all my best intentions abandoned me, and I called my son an imbecile. I regret it and it shames me. How peculiar relations between fathers and sons are! No amount of energy applied seems to lead to improvement. I, who've always said I know nothing about painting, was angry because my son was shouting the same thing.

The others acted even worse. "I would say an artist who doesn't appeal to the many is on the wrong track," said Valentino, ever the slow and solemn administrator.

Alfio had such contempt for Valentino's opinion that he didn't reply. Antonia, unhappy about her husband's second conversational gambit, after the first had come to such a bad end, tried to warn him of the danger by tugging on his sleeve. But Valentino, all unaware, straightened his jacket, studying it with curiosity to see why it was pulling. Now Alfio, after hesitating a moment, said to his sister, "Let him speak. What harm can he do me?"

Soon another grave offense would come to join this new one. After he had eaten, Orazio wanted to see the painting. Alfio announced that he did not wish to be present, and went to his room. But then he couldn't resist the punishment, and just when Orazio, standing before the picture, began to laugh, one hand on the belly he didn't really have, Alfio appeared at the doorway of my study, leaned against the doorjamb, and began to gaze intently, not smiling by any means, but sufficiently in control of himself that he didn't seem to be suffering. "From houses to horses," said Orazio, who had in fact discovered, beneath one of the houses, something that resembled the face of a horse.

From that day forward, my relations with Alfio worsened. I did everything I could to improve things, except that I was unable to tell him I liked his pictures. He'd called me an idiot, even if only as regards to painting. I couldn't now say to him, "Yes I'm an idiot, if only in the field of painting." I courted him, I gave him money, I patted him, and I kissed him on the cheek, innumerable times, while he kissed the air. It was all for naught, because I never dared to speak to him about painting. "Did you paint well this morning?" I asked one day when I met him coming home with his map and his paints. "I do my best," he said, hurrying off. He was quite frightened I might ask to see some of his work.

His reserve was hard to bear. All the theories that I had derived from my relations with my father were useless here, because I had behaved quite differently with my father. Nevertheless, I continued to be kind and courteous. When there was a disagreement at table, I always sided with Alfio. When he asked me for money, I gave without batting an eyelid. I spoke only gentle words to him. I probably seemed strange and not very affectionate. While I embraced him, a voice inside shouted, "What a good man I am, what a good man!" The conviction that we're good probably makes us far less good.

I suspect we never achieved better relations because he really didn't care much how we got along. Many a time I asked him to keep me company, but he always managed to get away as soon as he could.

He developed passionate friendships first with one, then another, of his artist colleagues. For some time he was utterly devoted to one who painted really beautiful portraits. I said, rather miffed, "Oh I see, so it's possible to paint things as they are too." He blanched as only he can, and said, "Everyone has his own personality." He (we) had been dealt that twisted personality with the disorderly colors. There was nothing to do but endure it. He managed to get his own back every time.

And so I reached the conclusion that if my dying and my death turned out to be a hard punishment for Alfio, it would be a punishment he deserved. I could therefore embark on death with peace of mind. Death is an adventure everyone undertakes and I must accept mine. I now had good reason to think that the consequences would not be overly serious: Augusta would mourn me without, however, losing control, Antonia wouldn't mourn me at all, and Alfio would follow my example, or do something else entirely, and it would be all the same to me.

II

My daughter's an estimable person, like her mother, and even more so; she's all too estimable. Physically she looks like her aunt Ada: she stands tall, her little head is elegant, and so is her figure. From what Augusta tells me, I know that she's pleasing to men, but when just a girl she took a vow to be virtuous, and she has remained true to it not only in her every act, but in her every word, and even her every glance. In short, her virtue is excessive. This may be the result of the fact that she did part of her schooling with the nuns, but I believe that heredity has left cells responsible for this exaggerated behavior in her very organism. I like to think she inherited the virtue from her mother and the exaggeration from me. I'm here alone before this sheet of paper that probably no one will ever see. So there's no reason either to laugh at me or to consider me presumptuous. Virtue was never strong in me, but desire was excessive. I believe I've made a major discovery about the laws of heredity, which could easily be investigated and verified. In Antonia, the principle is clear: she inherited from her mother the quality of virtue, and from her father the measure in which that quality would be manifest. As it happens, I'm excessively modest. It was my daughter's misfortune that Augusta's good qualities were dosed out for Antonia by me.

Even when she was a girl, life was a series of duties. Studies, it must be said, were never her strong suit. She never learned even one foreign language and mastered none of the sciences. But she was a saint. The nuns adored her and made her life as pleasant as possible. There was a time when she even thought she wished to enter monastic life. Augusta and I spent some terrible hours worrying that this was also what the nuns wanted, thinking that they would certainly be victorious. You hear so much about how the great monastic orders are keenly interested in attracting postulants. But the good sisters wouldn't hear of it, and they helped us to dissuade our daughter Antonia from taking such a step. As I write this it occurs to me that maybe they had studied Antonia and realized that she would be as much of a bore in the convent as she is at home today.

However, when she was a girl she was a joy to us, a joy enhanced by our admiration for her purity; and, on my part, there was also a certain amusement at the strange product sprung from my blood.

Antonia was dead set against the freedoms permitted to young ladies after the war. Not only wasn't she interested in dancing, she wouldn't leave the house by herself. She had to be accompanied everywhere by her mother or one of the maids, and the assignment of these duties was a real domestic problem, given the amount of surveillance she condemned us to. Sometimes even I had to leave home in the evening to take her somewhere, or fetch her. She was like a small bale of goods that could only be moved by a shipping agent.

And she defended this elective bondage of hers as sharply as Alfio did his painting. When she spoke about other young ladies, she sounded like a spiteful old woman, and hearing her made you forget that her face was fresh and her eyes sparkling with youth.

However, this desire to be tucked away in a sturdy strongbox did show that she considered herself something precious, a jewel. In fact she dedicated great attention to the adornment of her little person, and her clothing consumed a fair share of the family budget. I suspect that Augusta also kept quiet about some portion of what our daughter cost, which can't have been difficult, because I never involve myself in money matters except when in very foul spirits and needing an outlet for my bile. Augusta in truth was like me, her moods changing with the weather vane. When she needed my help to guide Antonia, she would be the first to complain about how much she cost us. If I should speak first, however, I would meet ironclad assertions that Antonia was entirely modest and cost no more than other young ladies in the same circles. This left me annoyed with both Antonia and Augusta, because it all seemed designed to put me in the wrong. Now that I am old, I find it hard to be in the wrong because I've erred or overlooked something, but quite enraging to learn that I'm in the wrong through no fault of my own, but on account of someone else's devious interference.

All these things, however, have been long forgotten. I mention them merely to help explain what was now happening.

When she was fifteen, Antonia had just one friend, a homely girl, thick-waisted and ill-built, with just one beautiful feature: dark eyes that gleamed with strange splendor and seemed to have been set in that head just to observe, admire, and envy the beauty of others. Marta Crassi,* she was, and willy-nilly she would become Antonia's sister-in-law. I say willy-nilly because Antonia had put herself in such a difficult position in society that she had no other option but to marry one of Marta's two brothers. Falling in love with an entire household: it was not, in truth, unheard of in my family. It wasn't much, but some pale traces of me do survive in the family.

Thinking that other more important traits might have been handed down, when the news came from Florence that Marta's brother Eugenio had been visiting Antonia when he was on leave and appeared ever more affectionate, I was sure that the young man was heading for an unhappy adventure. But we shall see how little I knew my own flesh and blood.

I loved poor Eugenio myself. Generous, never calculating his own interests, fired up with notions about humanity and his country, he left Trieste and enlisted in the Italian army. While he was living in Trieste he had never revealed his interest in Antonia to anyone. I suppose that when he could escape the trenches to visit his sister,

---

*In *Umbertino*, Eugenio and Valentino's sister is called Clara. It's unclear whether the lapsus is Svevo's or Zeno's.

where Antonia was also to be found, falling in love came easy, for Antonia's sitting room was in any case certainly preferable to the trenches. I do not know whether the two young people spoke of love. Augusta, who knows her daughter's mind, is sure they didn't. She says Antonia would not have spoken of love without insisting they discuss marriage, and that sounds about right.

But I'm convinced there was love, because when Eugenio died, Antonia agreed immediately to engage herself to be married to his brother Valentino, who was considerably less lovable. That hasty decision was a clear declaration of love for the deceased. Poor Antonia! What an inferior surrogate she had to live with!

Eugenio had rushed off to Italy to serve his country, tossing aside all thoughts of himself. The Austrian bonds recently inherited from his father he had deposited with a bank, and thought no more about it. And so when the enemy abandoned their trenches, thanks in part to his own participation, he had unwittingly destroyed his own means. A magnificent example of heroism—and absentmindedness. Then, a few days before the armistice, he tripped on a mine and was horribly ripped to shreds and died.

Poor Valentino (poor indeed, because now he too is dead) had also volunteered, but the trenches didn't agree with him and he somehow found a way to withdraw from the lines as far as Milan, where he found a good job with an insurance company. God knows I don't wish to speak ill of him, but he was not a suitable husband for my dear daughter. Fat and faintly unhealthy-looking: that was the impression I had of him when I saw him after the war, before his marriage to my daughter, when I said to Augusta, "Can this be the husband for our beautiful Antonietta?"

Augusta shrugged her shoulders, resigned; she hadn't been the one to choose him. Then, not wanting to rock the boat and wishing everyone could be in harmony, she added, "He has promised to undertake a slimming regime. And if you look at him carefully, you'll see he's not homely."

I did my best to get accustomed to him. He was so categorically certain of his own opinions. The most cheering good news, in his telling, became tedious and dull, whether for the nasal sound of his voice or for the air of great importance he assumed as he undertook to tell us. And he knew everything about the subject—he knew it from every angle, and with the utmost precision. So that any topic he spoke on became a lesson. With time I learned to pay attention to that voice I had first tried to escape. So as not to have to endure it at length, one had to accept it immediately, willingly, follow and remember every twist and turn. He wouldn't release me until I had mastered everything.

But I don't wish to speak too unkindly of him. First, he was the father of my dear Umbertino, and second, he left Antonia with a pretty penny.

I only meant to say that I never understood how Antonia could have fallen for him. Or why she remained so attached to him, never thinking of betraying him even though the slimming regime he undertook was a failure. The evolution of the flesh is certainly a grand mystery. When I hear that history repeats itself, I don't find it hard to believe. It repeats itself, but where it will appear, we don't know. That's the surprise! A second Napoleon could come forth from my house, and I wouldn't be at all surprised. And everyone would say "History repeats itself," when in fact nothing in the world had paved the way for it.

All of a sudden, last year, Valentino's large body began to shrivel, although he lost no weight, his face turned livid, and he began to breathe like a fish out of water, sometimes quite rowdily, almost shouting. Dr. Raulli understood right away that his condition was serious, and informed us. Antonia settled in beside her husband's bed and didn't move from there until he died.

My nephew Carlo told us what the illness was: premature aging. "Quite suddenly, in a matter of weeks, his organism becomes what yours is today, dear uncle. But what you're capable of tolerating at seventy, he, just forty, cannot. You need less air, less vigorous circulation; everything in you is less alive. But you're able to keep on living... nonetheless."

None of this seemed at all logical to me. But I didn't object, rather

I withdrew into myself, into my aged organism, to protect it from all these indignities and keep on living... nonetheless. What did any of them know about life? My mind is livelier now than poor Valentino's ever was. I don't get myself all tangled up in some matter of virtually no importance, analyzing it well beyond what it deserves, and dropping it only when the company around me is half dead of boredom. That ought to be the proof that my respiration is more vigorous than his ever was. Now they complain I am distracted, that I don't remember names and faces. But these are failings I've always had, and if they're an old man's failings it means that I was able to tolerate old age from birth, while Valentino died at forty years.

When he was dead, we were astounded by Antonia's show of grief. At first we all admired her. We were moved to tears, and her displays were such that I can say I have never wept so much over a dead man as I did over Valentino. Even Carlo and Alfio, the two young ones who'd most ridiculed Valentino's sluggish, heavy ways, put aside their antipathy to remember him fondly through Antonia's grief. Who knew more of him than his widow? Destiny had struck her a terrible blow. Everyone wanted to help her, sympathize with her.

But when a week had gone by Carlo began to complain, seeing that Antonia's grief, rather than diminishing, became more and more elaborate in word and deed, so that everyone and everything was obliged to be in mourning, not just Antonia and Umbertino (who looked incredibly cheerful doing his somersaults in black), but Augusta and Alfio and me and my automobile, and every day Antonia found new reasons to weep greater downpours and oblige us to torture ourselves, squeezing more tears from now parched ducts. Carlo had been so kind that first week that Antonia missed him, and then developed a rancor that even Alfio shared at first. But soon Alfio's grief ran out. It was no match for his sister's. And so there was only myself, Augusta, and Antonia to mourn poor Valentino. Antonia wept louder to make up for the missing mourners. She began to coin phrases to speak more eloquently of the unprecedented catastrophe that had befallen her, and one of her phrases wounded me deeply. Each day, as soon as she saw me, she'd say, "Before it killed him, the fates dishonored him by aging him so much." Now I too withdrew, offended. Old age a dishonor! Such a thing could only have been said after the world war. Afterwards I had to tell Augusta why I'd been absent, and Augusta told Antonietta, who didn't wait for me to come back to mourn with her, but found a pretext to come and lay all her grief on me. This tragedy was extremely useful to her as an outlet for tears but it left me a twisted rag, unsure where my head was, or my feet. She threw herself at my knees, all in black and draped in veils, and weeping and wailing she said that old age, in which I prospered, had been deadly for Valentino. Apparently this allowed her to insist that my old age was in no way dishonorable, while Valentino's had been a disgrace.

And once again I was moved, as if Valentino had just died that very moment. I lifted her up, embraced her, and for several days, wanting to help the poor girl, so innocent and so unfortunate, I stayed with her to mourn. I even felt my paternal spirit reviving and I searched my soul for grief and pity, hoping to wash away my remorse at having wounded her. Never had I loved sad Valentino so much as in those days: Valentino, who after a life half dead was now fully dead, although in both the first case and the second he had inspired great affection.

One evening, late, after supper, a scene I shall never forget took place. It was early September. It was still quite hot and Augusta, Antonia, and I were under the pergola in front of the house, from where you could once look out on the city and the port, and now could see only a glint of faraway sea behind huge, squalid military barracks. After repeating her highly original theory about honorable and dishonorable old age, Antonia kept sobbing, her head resting on my shoulder. Her tears were altogether a sharper weapon than her words. Augusta too was crying, but I knew she was far away. She wasn't grieving for Valentino as we were. Not long before, I had once again explained how I thought Antonia was misusing us badly and would disturb my last years on earth with her mourning. Augusta didn't know that I had since made my peace with my daughter, and I could find no way to tell her. She was weeping about the tension between us. She had wept over Alfio's painting too, not the picture itself, but the tension it had caused between my son and me. She despised tension, the tension that was inevitable between human beings, and especially inevitable between fathers and sons, but which she had been able to eliminate from her large company of dogs, cats, and birds, to whom she gave the better part of her life.

A solitary wino went by singing on the path that leads by the house and then runs up the mountain. I knew him well. Wine electrified the musical instinct in him and he gave himself to it in an innocent, leisurely way. I'd watched him many times. He had only two old popular songs in his quite restricted repertoire, to which he would make small variations, so slight that his inspiration never seemed muddled. Nor was his voice at all muddled, merely gentle, frail, and very tired. What a fine fellow he was, so happy about the wine he had guzzled. And so modest! To put on such a concert without an audience.

And so Antonietta wept and I reflected on that wino who had so effortlessly solved the problem of living. By day, work. By evening (not night), music! His soft notes grew fainter as he moved off, and then faded away.

"Poor thing!" Antonietta sobbed.

"Who?" I snapped, fearing greatly that she was still talking of Valentino.

"That poor fellow singing so sadly on the path," she mumbled. "He's lost someone and is consoling himself with wine, I reckon."

The idea that anyone who drank too much did so because he or she had lost someone seemed quite exaggerated to me, although perhaps it would be more plausible if one had statistical tables to hand. And yet I was very pleased that she had spoken of the poor lonely warbler rather than her deceased husband. I rested my shoulder lightly against hers, and, impulsively generous, suggested she leave her empty house and come with Umbertino to stay with us. At first she rebuffed the idea so violently that I didn't dare to insist. But Augusta had looked up, her face washed clean of any discouragement. She saw an agreement in the making and agreement was her main purpose in life. She suffered when others abandoned Antonia in her grief; she wished they would all sit around the table mourning with her for eternity. A few months later she, too, lost her patience, not because she had no more tears to cry, but because her daughter had no love for the animals Augusta looked after; she wanted to banish them from the house. Our daughter detested those dogs and cats because among other things, they don't observe mourning. A dog will sniff at the dead remains of one of his companions out of curiosity. Taken aback for a moment, he'll then bound off, delighted that such a thing has not happened to him.

That first evening we didn't progress beyond Antonia's tears and protests: She would never leave the house where he died! And where in our house would she find a place for the furniture he had acquired with such love and from which she would never be parted?

But Augusta did not lay down her weapons. First she convinced me that we had no use anymore for the ground floor, which we had once used for receptions, and that after properly refitting it, we could give it to Antonia. I wasn't at all opposed, having already compromised myself by offering to host her, carried away as I was by the touching song of my dear, drunk friend. Augusta had the space measured to see whether Valentino's gargantuan, heavy furniture could fit in this new home. It did, although there was less space for people to move around.

Antonia, with rare stubbornness, refused every proposal, and each offer was a new occasion for loud weeping and wailing.

Then, on precisely the nineteenth of the month—the third or fourth month after Valentino expired—she changed her mind. That morning we were told that she wanted to go to the cemetery. We went to fetch her with the automobile. She was surprised that Alfio hadn't come along. I explained that Alfio was not feeling well. In addition, Augusta added, he was obliged to stay at home because he was expecting a friend. So there was a double reason for him not to come, which caused Antonia such bitterness that, for a little while that day, her grief was less insistent. She was making order around the grave, decking it with flowers. We were waiting for Carlo, who had promised to come if he could get away from the hospital, but we would wait in

vain. When all hope of seeing him vanished, Antonia stopped dis-
tributing flowers and gave vent to all her grief in our arms.

It was a slightly misty autumn day, a day when the midday sky is
quite bright but not luminous, the color of quicklime. I always think
you can see everything better on such days: the cypresses, the tombs
with their engravings and figures, the boundary wall, and the dark
chapel. I was struck by this effect, and before noting it down here, I
spoke to Alfio, who had been out painting that day. "Perfect indirect
lighting," was his succinct judgment. "Ideal!" I had moved away to
be slightly more comfortable, but I hadn't forgotten my little girl
heaving in my wife's arms. Under her veils her pretty face, though
pale, shone with youth and energy. She was weeping copiously, and
we had to look after her, but there was little doubt she was doing
better than we were. Someone who looked like Carlo was approaching the gate. He had just his way of walking, very upright yet somehow
negligent: his pace lazy, nose in the air and glasses shiny. "Carlo!" I
shouted. Antonia stopped crying for an instant and stared at him
too. "No, it's not Carlo," she said. And in fact the young fellow passed
by, inspecting us rather curiously.

Now Antonia quieted down and pretty soon we left the cemetery.
She was silent for a long time in the car, her bloodshot eyes trained
on the road, which undoubtedly she could not see. Then suddenly
she turned to Augusta and asked where in our house her servants'
quarters would be, after she had moved in. Augusta told her. Once
again she turned her lovely eyes to the invisible road for a moment,
and when she returned to us, she murmured, "I would like to try. If
you find I'm disturbing you or I become aware I'm in the way, I'll
return to my own house."

And that was how she decided to come live with us. And when I
think of her in that quicklime light, her little face still marked with
childish lines, that dimple on her chin, I think, "My darling little
hellcat, you want to weep so much, but you don't want to weep alone."

However, it was on account of her move that I came to know
Umbertino better, and he became more and more important to my
life.

UMBERTINO

I AM A man born in inopportune times. In my youth, only the old were respected, and let me say that in those days the old did not permit the young so much as to talk about themselves. They made them hold their tongues even when the subject at hand was by all rights theirs: for example, love. I remember one day when my father and his contemporaries were talking about a wealthy gentleman of Trieste, who had conceived a grand passion and was ruining himself as a consequence. They were a group of men aged fifty and upwards, who out of respect for my father allowed me to join them. I was affectionately called "the young colt."

I naturally had the consideration for my elders that my times demanded, and I looked forward eagerly to learning even about love from them. But at one point, not sure I understood, I broke into the conversation: "Well, in my experience—" My father promptly interrupted. "Oh, now even the fleas want to scratch."

And now that I am old, only the young are respected: in short, I've gone through life without ever being granted any consideration. This must account for a certain antipathy I feel toward the young who are respected today, as well as toward the old respected back then. I feel I'm alone in the world, where even my age has always been a mark of inferior status.

I believe that one reason I adore Umbertino is that he has no age. He's seven and a half and as yet he as none of our vices. He doesn't love and he doesn't hate. His father's death provoked more curiosity than suffering. I heard him, on the same evening his father died, surprised, inquisitive, ask his nursemaid, "So I could even kick a dead man and he wouldn't be angry?" He had no intention of kicking his father to avenge himself for the man's long-winded lessons. He merely wanted to know. Life to him is a spectacle, quite detached, from which neither good nor evil threatens (so long as it doesn't land right on him); it's just a source of information.

I began to care for him early, when I saw him only from time to time. I used to go once a day to visit my daughter and son-in-law, and I watched our little hero, blond and handsome, grow. He had two negative qualities I liked: he didn't want to recite the verses he had learned by heart in front of strangers, and he didn't like to be kissed by people he didn't know. I didn't kiss him and I didn't care about his verses. Every day I brought him the same small box of sweets. I didn't yet love him enough to want to surprise him with new presents, and on my way to visit I would always stop for a moment, mechanically, in the same nearby shop. I saw he was waiting somewhat impatiently for my present. One day he surprised Antonia, showing her that if you put all those boxes together you could make a house, a house for Grandfather, if you cut away part of his body, or rather his entire body minus the head. The little man studied my head and then the house, to judge the proportions. "Do you really want to kill Grandfather?" Antonia objected. "He won't be able to breathe with just his head."

The little one studied me for a moment. "Can't you see he uses only his head to breathe?"

The child's lavish imagination was too much for me. I passed an anxious night, and my anxiety transformed Umbertino's idea into a horrendous dream. My body had been cut away and all that was left of me was my head, sitting on a table. I could still talk, and I put up with it all in a spirit of satisfying Umbertino's every whim. But my breathing was necessarily limited, and left me with a short-winded greed for air, and I wondered, "How long will I have to go on breathing this way until my body grows back?"

I was so impressed by this nightmare that I could not chase it from my mind for a whole day. I went so far as to think, "One simply mustn't put up with a life in which such monstrous things are imaginable."

And yet it had been that little blond head imagining.

I'd be hard pressed to reproduce even one of the sounds that Umbertino used to make, to illustrate their charm and subtlety. Although I understood them, I don't recall them. I do remember that I smiled at them. And I remember something I discovered about him: Umbertino's face grows very expressive when he is at a loss for words. His great big, bright blue eyes open ever so wide to see better, then shut in intense concentration, and then he takes a sidelong glance that lends a traitorous look to his rosy face, searching for the word in some corner, or looks upward, as if seeking aid from the heavens. Yes! The absence of words brings forth all his expressiveness. And I adore what I learn. Little by little I've discovered an Umbertino not everybody knows, which is all the more reason to love him. All around me—I know this because I see everything—they grumble that I see, hear, and understand less and less. That may be, but what I do see and hear leads me to very interesting discoveries.

Since he's been living with me, Umbertino has been a nuisance at times. The house is large but he has found nowhere in it to stay more pleasant than my study, and he is always there, somewhat in the way. My books were finally being used; he needed them to build pyramids. What a mess! He wanted the gramophone on, but unlike other enthusiasts he always found the record too long. If he can reach it with his hands he'll stop it, and if he could break it, he would. The first time I prevented him from touching it, he said to me in all innocence, "Grandfather, why don't you go away?" He's so convinced that any limitation of his freedom is an injustice that he imagines I'm in my own home by chance, not by right. That child is a genuine protest against his father. I honestly think that sometimes heredity is no more than an impatient shrug that tosses aside the old stock and invents something entirely new. I don't enjoy being at home alone with Umbertino. When the child is alone and has nothing to do, he becomes quite aggressive. I'm no good at telling stories. Poor Valentino (with that imagination!) could talk to him for hours. At times I listened to those stories. The child sat stock still in his father's arms, gazing at the mouth spilling out tales that sent him into raptures. Antonia, herself rapt, said to me, "That's the fifth time he's heard the same story." It was he who wanted to hear that story, about the fairy who goes to visit all the children to choose the best of them, and finds that the best is one of those who always thought himself the worst. We adults grow impatient and interrupt if someone tells us a story for the second time. But my boy always demanded that the thing be repeated. When the fairy strolls through the woods, the trees bow down in greeting. And the child bowed down, a tree himself, amused, whether at night or under the bright daytime sun. At night he opened his eyes wide to avoid any obstacles; by day he half shut them so as not to be hurt by the strong light. This was the child everyone believed to be a naughty boy, while instead he was full of a goodness no one recognized, and that only a fairy could reveal. Valentino's sad recitation was essential. Without it, Umbertino wouldn't react. That sad recitation had real efficacy. The man opened his big mouth, and consequential words emerged that instantly materialized into things and persons.

By the time Umbertino came to us, he had discovered a way to make up for his father's absence. He simply told the stories himself. He knew—I believe—just two, and I can't repeat them because I never bothered to listen. Once I sat though one, observing the intriguing gestures of his struggle with words, and he looked at me to see if I'd enjoyed the tale and asked, "Did you like that? Do you want me to tell it again?" I proposed he tell it again, and I would read, write, or play the violin. No, I had to stay and listen, otherwise the story wouldn't seem real to him. So I would try to stay and listen, but the usual perturbation began to rise in my breast: "What a good man I am, what a good man." And in order to get on with my own affairs, I'd hand him over to Renata.

Renata is a dear little dark-haired girl from Friuli. An orphan. She's been with us four years and she's only eighteen. She's one of those girls who became a woman during the war, and so didn't have to lengthen her short skirts, which in earlier times were worn only by little girls. She isn't well educated, nor does she observe and discover things as I do, but perhaps because she's close to being a child herself she puts up with Umbertino's chatter better. From my room—the stubborn boy never wanted to be far from it—I could hear his child-ish voice, interrupted from time to time by the girl's frank, fresh, irrepressible laugh.

But then Umbertino and I came to an agreement. At home we would meet only at luncheon, but each morning he would come out with me for an hour's walk before breakfast. This arrangement com-plied with Dr. Raulli's recommendation that I take an hour of exer-cise every day. When faced with walking, Umbertino told no stories, but placed his dear soft little hand in my large rough one. And I had to be careful to keep a firm hold on that hand, because Umbertino often stumbled; his eye was drawn by many things: a distant wall, half in ruins, the tramcars marked with numbers that he knew how to read, the train with its puffing locomotive, sometimes nearby, sometimes far away, although his eye never fell on the little impedi-ments in his way, the puddles into which his feet would sink, were I not paying attention.

What a lot of things the boy saw! Always the same things, because on account of my weak lungs outings in this city could never be very long, for once in the country one is already in the mountains. A night's sleep seemed to revive Umbertino so much that every single thing was new to him in the morning. So new that it looked new to me too. A railway track! Why did he stare at it like that? Why did he want to follow it? As long as it demanded no effort, I followed it too, to please him. But when we had to walk on the gravel between the tracks, or the railroad ties were too far apart to jump from one to the other, I grew impatient and dragged the boy away. Still, he kept on gazing at the tracks. They were the base upon which the great train glided along so mysteriously. And it was important to discover where they began, because every starting point is important, and it was also quite disturbing not to be able to see that other important part of the track, the end. I laughed and suggested that he see in that stretch not the track's beginning but its end. It was a revolutionary idea to him, and he hesitated before it. And then he saw, he understood! Yes indeed, this was the end of the track.

One day we climbed up on a wall and watched an amusing scene below. A mad horse had got free in the courtyard down there and a strapping big youth was trying to get him back in the stable. The horse was rearing and kicking the air. Umbertino, safe on his wall, was enjoying himself immensely, just shrieking with pleasure. His noisy excitement certainly cheered me, yet I also feared it might be a symptom of that hysteria that so infected his ancestors. However, his excitement could do no harm here, because the poor devil struggling with the horse down below could neither see nor hear us. Then the young fellow had a bright idea. He ducked into a door that opened onto the courtyard and emerged with a bunch of hay in his hand. The horse nuzzled it, and when the youth drew back toward the same door, the animal followed him, docile now from hunger, and disappeared after him. Umbertino was shouting, "Don't do it! You're a fool, he'll capture you!" And every time we passed that place he'd eye "the courtyard of the foolish horse," as he called it. But we never saw either the man or the horse again. In Umbertino's mind, the struggle had maybe happened again, and this time the horse didn't allow himself to be caught, and delivered a few kicks, and now he is free and far, far away in some lovely pasture.

Why do I get so much pleasure out of Umbertino's childish fun? Now that I'm trying to collect my thoughts on this page in front of me, remembering Umbertino walking alongside on his short, slightly wobbly legs, it seems to me that irrational joy is always irrationally distributed among men.

.Joy is plentiful in infants, who are beatifically ignorant—and in this respect alone can be considered fairly rational. When as children we begin to investigate that colossal machine we've been given, life—those tracks that end where they begin—we don't yet comprehend the connection between life and us, and we consider it objectively and even joyously—the joy interrupted by flashes of pure terror. Adolescence is harrowing; we begin to discover that the machine is meant to devour us, and cannot decide where in the middle of that infernal contraption one can safely place a foot. Peace of mind came late to me, maybe because my illness made my adolescence go on longer than normal, while all around me my peers were quite oblivious, like the miller who sleeps peacefully next to his mill race while the wheel turns, squealing. But peace of mind, composed of resignation and still lively curiosity, comes to all in the end, and now as I walk beside Umbertino I'm very like him. We're well matched. His tender foot keeps him from finding my pace too slow, and the weakness of my lungs levels out our differences. He's content because the machine delights him, and I'm at peace too—not because I believe life can no longer hurt me, death being at hand to free me (for the truth is that up to now I've always kept death at arm's length, except once in a while in my mind), but because I'm so accustomed to the machine by now that I'm only frightened if I think that people are actually better than I've judged them, or that life is more serious than it has always appeared to me. Then the blood rushes to my head as if I were about to do a somersault.

Poor Umbertino! The unexpected frights get in the way of his contentment and his curiosity. He's famous in the family for a show of such fear some years back. He had trouble going to sleep in the dark, and his mother was seeking to convince him that there was nothing to be afraid of because there are no lions at this latitude, and what is more all our windows and doors were tightly sealed. But he complained that it was the men who slipped in through the cracks that worried him. It was an important discovery that windows and doors can never be sealed so tightly that danger is unable to get in.

At times he even exaggerates the real dangers of this world. Once, he was given some new shoes, shiny shoes with buckles. To put his mind at rest he wanted to sleep with the shoes on, and I will never forget the sight of that little man, all hot with sleep, lying on his back with his bare feet in his shoes, splayed out on the bed. Not even in sleep did he let his guard down. But it's clear that life is kinder than he imagined, if other people feel free to remove their boots before crawling into bed.

A boy of three is a toy that everyone wants to play with. You press a button at the bottom and right away the top begins to move. I regret to say I once interfered with the workings of that toy myself.

I'd been invited to dinner by Valentino, and I arrived so early that

I found Umbertino still at the table, eating an apple after his meal. I quickly took another from the basket of fruit and pretended I had extracted it from his throat so he would think it was the one he had already eaten. Surprised and frightened, the little one began to eat that apple too, since it was his, and I said nothing, as if it were obvious it was. And when I extracted the second apple from his throat I was disposed to let him eat that one too. But the boy refused it, his small stomach feeling none of the relief he ought to have had from my tricks.

I forgot all about this episode, until Augusta and I were getting ready to leave. Antonia wanted us to see the child asleep in his bed. He was sleeping in a cot sealed on the sides with netting. No one gave a second thought to turning on the light, because everyone knew that when Umbertino fell soundly asleep there was no danger of waking him up. He had thrown himself against the netting and his head was resting on that instead of his pillow. His cheeks were on fire and he was breathing faster than usual—or so it seemed to me. Antonia bent over to straighten him out and he allowed himself to be moved, murmuring "I ate it—and poof!—it was whole again." Antonia laughed. "Hallucination courtesy of his grandfather." My heart, though, was a little heavy.

I think I understand. He's something of a worrier, Umbertino. In his brief existence, he has already been threatened, and also punished. Now fear is an emotion lodged in the flesh. It works like a protective envelope, enclosing a body even before it's exposed to the air. It can be misleading perhaps, but certainly also a safeguard. And little Umbertino is afraid of lions, although there are no lions, and of carabinieri, who have never taken the least notice of him, and who we hope never will. When he sees one, he falls silent. He knows their job is to police, and that they are tougher than the surveillance he's already subject to, which is thorough, slightly tedious, but delivered with sweets and affection. It's not out of the question that lions might appear in Trieste some time or other, or that this child, who sometimes provokes his father's and his grandfather's anger and makes his mother cry, might come to the attention of the carabinieri one day.

His grandfather's bouts of ire never lasted long and were soon followed by gentle explanations and reprimands addressed to myself as well as to him, but always in remarks that portrayed me as doting, never ashamed. We walked very easily together along the streets of the city, I far less absentminded than he because I was always alert to real automobiles that could threaten him, or to admiring glances aimed at this child with a head full of foolish thoughts. In this, then, I resembled him less, but only in this, only in that I wasn't free but enslaved to the job of surveillance. Otherwise we'd have walked along looking very much alike, often silent, because Umbertino is already used to not saying everything that comes into his head. The last time we were together, he hid in the shade of a tree to enjoy how he then ceased to cast a shadow. He squeezed himself farther under the tree, drawing in an arm which had been protruding. He succeeded, and then we continued on his way in silence. Perhaps he felt his thoughts were too childish to reveal.

After Antonia and Umbertino settled in, another nuisance often came to visit, a nuisance but also a prospect: Signor Bigioni. Not Baglioni and not Grigioni, as the other two friends who had been our familiars years back were called, but Bigioni. Whenever I address him he has to volunteer his name because I'm always unsure which is his among the three names, a fact that complicates our relations. I don't find him very sympathetic; he has some of Valentino's peculiarities. When he has an opinion, he's very sure of it, and he declares it, comments on it, and illustrates it with quite concrete, sometimes offensive, figures of speech. Once, confiding in me, he apologized for the fact that the moment Valentino died he'd honored his memory by seeking to marry his wife, although, as he explained, he knew very well that in doing so he showed himself to be a poor friend. And yet he felt it was compensated by the enormous generosity Valentino had shown him—it reminded him, he explained, of the sailor who, after several weeks on the open sea, adrift with his friend on a raft, dies, and saves the other by becoming his dinner. Having thought up this atrocious comparison and told it to me, he was ready to repeat it to Antonia too. That metaphor explained everything, and he was convinced it was important to explain everything in this world.

I was the first to recognize this nascent hope and prospect. Right away I spoke to Carlo, who's frequently around these days. Carlo, always so sure of himself, said that miracles don't repeat themselves in this world.

"What miracles?" said I, surprised.

"The miracle of Valentino marrying Antonia."

I was offended. What miracle was there in a young man marrying one of the most beautiful women in Trieste? She'd been the joy of our family, that pretty little girl, our jewel, admired by all our friends, and even today when they speak of her they call her beautiful, beautiful like her aunt Ada, while Ada's daughter, who lives in Buenos Aires, is homely like Ada's sister Augusta, my dear wife Augusta. Every creature is made up of both ugliness and beauty, and must be granted the time to manifest all aspects.

To repay the offense I told Carlo of Bigioni's proposal, which I'd promised not to discuss with anyone besides Antonia. Carlo was so taken aback that he lost hold of his cigarette and it fell on the ground. He began to laugh: So miracles did repeat themselves! From then on, all of us, including Carlo, were more tolerant of Bigioni's company. We all rallied round him protectively, we put up with him and loved him, apart from Antonia and Umbertino.

Bigioni (what an excellent idea to write down that name again and again) behaved like the person he is, blind to anything but his own desires.

We were on our way back from the cemetery, Carlo, myself, and Bigioni, having buried poor Valentino. In the carriage, Bigioni behaved impeccably. He spoke of nothing but his long friendship with Valentino and mourned his premature death with feeling. "What am I going to do without him?" he said. At this point, however, I'm sure I saw him smile. I'm certain of it. At the time I interpreted this as a mere nervous contraction of the mouth because it didn't seem the moment to smile. It was pouring with rain and we were all soaked. Valentino was scarcely beneath the sod. I myself had even smiled slightly thinking of Valentino, just arrived in his tomb and mobbed by the dead who'd gotten there first, saying in his characteristic way,

"Slow down everyone, take it easy." But such an out-of-place smile exhibited by me could never be interpreted as malicious. While Bigioni, after smiling, smoothed his thick blond beard with evident pleasure and passed a hand over his bald head. Gestures that reminded me of a wild animal showing satisfaction after an abundant meal, and which I puzzled about until Bigioni decided to choose me to confide in. He meant to marry the wife of the dead man, and had therefore begun by taking a place in the family carriage.

In some ways, it was foolish of him to swear me to secrecy while imparting his confidences, when by mistake he had already alerted no less than Umbertino to his plans that very day, when the boy was still drenched after the downpour at his father's funeral. Their vast house now seemed almost empty. Just before the service it had been invaded by a mob of friends and relatives who had left us in the rain at the cemetery to come back alone. Bigioni gazed around contentedly. Look how much space there was for him there, even too much! He was feeling so sure of himself that I wouldn't be surprised if he was even planning to sublet a portion as soon as it was his.

Then, seeing that Umbertino was in tears—Antonia had upset him by forbidding him to play on the day of his father's funeral—Bigioni pulled the child to him and kissed him (although Umbertino was doing his best to get free of that tramp, albeit a well-combed tramp, not at all bristly), and told the boy he should be happy it was raining.

It was a sign that the heavens had opened wide to receive his poor father.

There's another Triestine saying I've heard, which says that fine weather, too, signals a hearty welcome in Heaven for the deceased. Fine people in this city. If it were up to them, all the dead would be royally received in Heaven.

The boy grew very grave. He had spotted a new machine to study, Heaven as Bigioni described it. Bigioni, seeing him so serious, wished to console him and blurted out, "So here you are, fatherless. How would you like to have a new father—for instance me?"

Umbertino would not forget those words. In the meantime, he

escaped from that tramp. And he did succeed, his mother present but unaware, at playing on the day of his father's funeral. He played with Heaven. For days and days Paradise was shut up tight and the dead were camped outside en masse waiting until it rained. As the first drops fell, the gates opened, and they all crowded in.

But Umbertino was not quite sure, and so he asked his mother, "If it's not raining when someone dies, are they condemned forever to wait at the gates and never allowed into Heaven?" Rousing herself from the torpor despair had cast her in, Antonia asked him what he meant. He told her, and she realized that Bigioni had disturbed and confused the poor child. She then turned kindly to Bigioni and begged him not to say such things to her son. Very kindly indeed, because up until then Bigioni hadn't seemed to be a contender for Valentino's estate but simply his closest friend—and therefore had to be treated better than anyone, better than her father, her mother, her brother, or her cousin.

Now Umbertino rid himself of that story of Heaven and the rain. Children have a great talent for forgetting. So that's how it is! There's no connection between rain and the gates of Heaven? Signor Bigioni was mistaken, and that was that.

However, there was still another puzzle. The second father. When he was getting into bed one night he asked his old nursemaid, "How many fathers can a person have in this world?" And the woman said one, unless you intend to be reborn. That concept of being reborn was also an appealing thought to play with. Umbertino slept on it and did not forget it. In the morning Antonia had her work cut out for her, removing all these eccentric ideas from that little head. And so she quickly learned of Bigioni's rash remark.

She did not forgive him. Bigioni was no longer considered Valentino's friend, but his enemy, and therefore also the enemy of the surviving wife, Antonia. She told me the following morning. In the midst of lengthy sobbing in my arms, she stopped and shouted, "This is my tremendous misfortune, that the worst that can befall a woman is exacerbated by every offense known to man." Then she told me what Umbertino had pretty accurately related. Her accusation was quite exaggerated. Every offense known to man? Poor Bigioni was guilty of just one offense: having proposed marriage so quickly. Let's draw a veil over that other exaggeration, that her misfortune was the worst that could befall a woman. A sufferer must be granted the satisfaction, let's even say the joy, of celebrating his or her pain. Even in a complaint like Job's, I can admire the sufferer's howl as a howl of magnificent joy.

At this point, I expected that poor Bigioni would meet with a flurry of kicks and be tossed out of the house. Nothing like that happened. He was the enemy but he had also been poor Valentino's friend, and so respect was due him. Everything that had the least connection with the deceased was not to be touched, and that included Bigioni, who smoked cigarettes with me, assisted Alfio with his painting, Carlo in his medical duties, and Augusta in looking after her animals. He was further permitted to speak to Antonietta about Valentino, but nothing else, and he was not to spend much time with Umbertino. I, for my part, put up with him unwillingly when he joined me on my excursions. As much as he tried, he didn't blend in with the young dreamer and the old dreamer. Out with him one day, we came to a point on the mountain above the tunnel into which Umbertino had once watched a train vanish. We'd passed by the tunnel not long before, and Umbertino had barely glanced at it. But above it now, he'd climbed up a wall and was gazing at that open mouth, seen from this new position for the first time. Bigioni didn't understand; he yawned. The boy had seen the tunnel close up just a little while ago and hadn't been interested. What was the point of choosing such an inconvenient and even dangerous spot, where I was obliged to watch out for him so zealously, just to see it from far away? But Umbertino was lucky. Suddenly a locomotive with its tender emerged from the tunnel, blasting its whistle. The boy began to squeal with pleasure, and Bigioni, startled, grabbed him by the jacket. "You see how he shies?" he said. The poor fellow had frequented mostly horses before he met Antonietta.

In short, he was not thrown out of the house. "I cannot be harsh with Valentino's friend, however much a traitor," Antonietta wept.

74 · ITALO SVEVO

She put up with him. What was odd was how she became harder and harder toward Bigioni as time passed and Valentino's death receded. After a while she barely replied to his "Buongiorno." At times she even pretended not to notice he was there. She seemed to be experimenting to see just how far she could go without actually tossing him out. Much as I don't like to speak ill of my only daughter, I must be frank here, if this account is to be worth anything: in my opinion, Bigioni's presence was convenient because it allowed Antonietta to expand and prolong her show of grief for poor Valentino. Her mourning would turn more violent when the fellow was there to bother her.

And I must admit, we all followed her example: studying how far we could go with him without actually throwing him out. Especially me. A few days after Valentino's death he came to speak to me and ask my advice. I listened with interest and curiosity, pretending I had not already heard it all from Antonia, who had in turn been informed by Umbertino. I followed the lead of Antonia, who believed that if he were to declare himself, she would have no choice but to throw him out of the house

I didn't mind at all listening to the man's story about wanting to marry just one woman in this world, just that one, and no other. Antonia had already dispelled any doubts I might have that Bigioni had a material interest in wanting to marry her. No, he was rich, much richer than Valentino, who had done business with him and knew his situation well. So then a breathless Bigioni began to tell me he had never been in love in his life. I pretended to believe him, because it's something I sometimes say of myself, and I always judge those who believe me to be courteous souls. But when I knew him better, I soon began to believe him. He really wasn't aware that there were other women in this world besides Antonia. You only had to walk down the street with him to be convinced. He just didn't see the armies of naked legs, embellished by silk stockings, on display.

He told me that he and Valentino, who was a little younger, had forged a close friendship in childhood. A selfish desire to get rich united them, and it seems they never had a place in their lives for expensive women who might compromise their reputations. They didn't actively object to them, they simply never considered them. They used to laugh at men who abandoned themselves to love without a thought for their good name or their future. How could they? All but recluses, both shunned society. Evidently it was only the untimely death of his brother that had led Valentino to find a wife; now his own death was leading Bigioni into the same adventure. The fellow told me quite ingenuously how much he had been affected by Valentino's marriage. The law that governed their two lives had been broken. He felt as free as the man who's made a pact with another to stop smoking when the second man breaks it. But how should he employ that freedom? Unable to face having to dig around in the great world for a wife, he continued to plod the route between his office, his home, and that of Valentino, and although he had decided to marry, hesitated. Visiting Antonia, he obviously met no suitable companion. While he hesitated, he fell in love with Antonia.

He swore he never imagined that Valentino could die, and certainly never hoped that he would. He was completely innocent of his death, but when it happened, he found he loved his friend far more dead than alive. Until then he'd felt nothing but admiration for Valentino's happiness. And now he insisted he wanted to marry Antonietta because she'd shown herself to be the true wife of a modest, hardworking fellow. But it was easy for me to see that he was deeply in love, and burned with hectic desire, inflamed by the obstacles he faced. Once, something like that happened to me. Today, however, after long experience, I find such delirium hard to fathom. Better to have women of all stripes: large, small, fair, and dark. I speak for those who deserve them, the young, the strong, and the handsome—who can be loved by them.

It was due to Bigioni that I thought at length about the one woman who could satisfy a man's desire: made in certain dimensions, blessed with a certain smile, a certain musical voice, a certain style of dress that she wears even when she is naked. I'm not so old, you see, if I can understand that.

And so my first conversation with Bigioni was fairly pleasant. He perused me as if his life depended on a single word of mine. And I perused him, guessing everything about him, and discovered he was faintly humiliated by having to depend so much on the wishes of others, a humiliation he accepted resignedly, not even dreaming of rebellion, accepting a cruel destiny. At the same time I was perusing myself somewhat nervously. Did I appear blind in seeming to understand nothing? But I thought I knew it all. It was only more difficult for me because, as I listened to him, I couldn't contemplate the same woman he did (my daughter), but had to find another woman on whom to carry out the experiment. So I pictured a large, beautiful woman—as Aretino, who should know, recommended—whom I sometimes meet and for whom I even get out my spectacles and shove them on my nose to see her better from afar. She's all harmony, strength, and abundance without excess, her foot, although not tiny, is well shod, her ankle in proportion, small. A woman, that is, equipped to be the only one for some time.

I understood, and so Bigioni's confidences pleased me. I had to temper his impatience, explain that in a family like ours, mourning was observed for a long time. Then it would be up to Antonia to decide. As for myself, I shook his hand willingly and cordially and promised him my help.

But then his confidences began to grow too frequent. Every single time Antonietta treated him coldly, he would come to see me. For a while I made myself available, because I thought he was about to leave our house for good, and I had my reasons for wanting to detain him. So I would stop the gramophone even if I had just turned it on, and resign myself to listening. To tell the truth, I'd follow the musical line of thought that I'd had to interrupt and let him go on talking. I'm perfectly capable of listening to someone talk without hearing a single word. It went very well. Of course the things he was telling me I already knew. In reply, I gave him what he expected: a firm handshake and a word of commiseration. But then his visits to my study became incessant. Antonietta's every act of indifference propelled him into my arms. He would come around, expecting me to turn off the gramophone or put down my book instantly. One day he appeared just as I'd succeeded in persuading Umbertino to leave. The boy had decided to investigate why the gramophone was shouting. I proposed to Bigioni that he talk to me while the music continued to play. I was listening to the Ninth Symphony, as I did every week, and it simply wasn't possible to interrupt music so sublime. I suggested he speak softly, promising him I'd hear every word. But he said nothing, waiting for the record to finish, and when I got up to change it began to speak. He couldn't bear it any longer. Whenever he arrived at the house, Antonietta would leave. And why? He asked nothing of her but to be permitted to grieve for her dear departed husband at her side.

In the short span of time it took me to change the record I managed to tell him that he'd been gravely imprudent when he confided in Umbertino. I stopped speaking when the music began; although I meant to listen to him, I had no intention of saying anything myself while the music was playing. He left very soon. He was certainly a proper friend to Valentino in musical matters. Except that Valentino had been deaf as a doornail and could listen to music for hours without the least show of impatience. He would smoke his long cigar, puffing in time to the music. Bigioni was more like a dog with sensitive ears. He grew very nervous and quickly escaped. I stroked my dear gramophone gratefully.

But he did not disappear, in spite of the fact that the others used similar techniques on him. Augusta always treated him very kindly, but she also abused him. She would send her little dog Musetta out with him, and once, when the dog had mange, she even obliged him to plaster the animal all over with ointment. Augusta considered this service a privilege. And not even this privilege discouraged Bigioni: he was so good to Musetta that she considered him one of the family.

Alfio, being Alfio, didn't employ such experiments, he simply did things that would drive the dishes off the table and the pictures off the walls, but had no effect on a living person like Bernardo Bigioni. One day Antonietta, who was suffering on account of her brother, spoke in Bigioni's hearing about Alfio, whose peculiar behavior and incomprehensible paintings were driving everyone crazy. Here at last was an opportunity to prove himself useful to the family. Bigioni undertook to reform Alfio with all the ardor he put into everything he hoped would make Antonietta appreciate him. I have no idea what he said to Alfio, but I happened to meet him in the little corridor outside Alfio's studio, just after he'd been in to see him, and he was mopping the sweat off his brow. That head of his—bare at the top but supplied with a great deal of hair around the bottom, right down to the neck—was always quite inclined to sweat.

Alfio did not change his painting style; what happened was that Bigioni changed his taste. He now wanted to buy one of Alfio's paintings at all costs. And he was more and more certain that they were beautiful. But Alfio stood firm. He insisted on being sure that anyone who bought one of his paintings ("wallow-works" was my name for them) really appreciated it. And then one day Bigioni came to me not to beg me to persuade Antonietta to love him, but merely to get Alfio to be his friend, and convince him to sell the poor man a picture. Well, I could no longer accuse Bigioni of being monotonous. And I was no longer bored having to listen to him. Quite the contrary. But his request upset me, because I realized I had no influence over anyone in my household. I couldn't make Antonia love him, and had to accept that this was not my vocation, nor could I make Alfio treat the poor fellow better. I could do nothing, and yet, feeling somewhat oppressed by my responsibility, to mollify Bigioni I proposed something that for a moment of wild naiveté seemed to me a fair compensation for Alfio's refusal. I proposed to sell him Alfio's picture, the one I kept hidden away in my drawer, for the same price it was sold to me. Bigioni, however, didn't even want to see the painting, and rushed off as if I'd begun to hum the Ninth Symphony, staring at me like a man who fears he's met a swindler. Now it seemed to me it was he who was rude, and I gazed at his back resentfully. Then I reconsidered. Bigioni wanted to buy Alfio, not his painting. If he bought a picture from me, he risked provoking Alfio to even greater fury.

I think Bigioni would have abandoned our house—a real house of torment for him—had it not been for Clara, Valentino's sister. After her brother died, Clara, who was a few years older than Antonia, used to come every afternoon and stay two hours with Antonia. At first I didn't like her much. To begin with, I didn't find her attractive; she was fat and solid and had thick, fleshy legs that would have done very well under one of those demure long skirts they used to wear in my day. Her eyes were lively and pretty, sometimes veiled with mischief when she smiled, but they did not belong to that body and made her seem even less pretty by contrast. But then, when I saw how good and kind she was, I came to love her myself. Augusta's affection was above all a matter of gratitude. That weeping daughter of hers was a real burden, and when Clara came, she was freed for an entire two hours. I never witnessed it myself, but I was told by Augusta that when Clara was present Antonia cried much less. I think I understand: a certain quantity of tears was due, and two people together filled the quota more quickly.

I appreciated her especially for how she handled Bigioni. I would have expected any sister of Valentino's to simply show him the door. Instead, she treated him firmly but politely. She spoke frankly to Antonietta, saying she expected a young woman like her would sooner or later remarry. And it would be better to marry Bigioni, a known friend of her deceased husband's, than someone else. Bigioni's mistake was to want what he didn't have a right to have with such haste. Clara's job, and all of ours, was to keep the fellow at bay so that he would be available when better times came.

I was enchanted. She was so much more practical than poor Antonietta, who knew nothing of the ways of this world. That was just the way to handle him! Surely she, too, suffered on account of her brother's death, but her lovely, powerful blue eyes always shone sharp and prudent. Yes, one had to take those eyes into account, because there's no such thing as seeing too well. Those eyes were clear-sighted even behind tears.

From then on, she was our favorite guest. When Antonietta's outbursts occurred in the morning, it was less of a nuisance because we knew that relief would soon arrive. And it always did. When we were notified of her arrival, Augusta and I, feeling greatly relieved, would follow her to Antonietta's room, as if part of a procession. She walked ahead, listening to and interrupting our complaints, reminding us how grave Antonietta's loss was. She took great care that everyone had the justice he or she deserved. Nearly every day we turned to her to sort out some problem with Antonietta, who was enraged because we'd given a dinner for old friends during the period of mourning, or objected because we'd expressed the wish that slowly she'd begin to remove some of her veils, for they would be terribly stifling now that summer was approaching. One day we were in the right, the next the balance tipped toward Antonietta. All of us submitted happily to Clara's judgment.

I often thought of that homely girl, from whom I learned that our instincts can never be eliminated, merely twisted toward ends they were not intended for. However attached she was to her brother—and that attachment was proved by the tears she shed every afternoon in Antonietta's company—she could not help but betray him by encouraging Bigioni's suit. It's simple enough: when people are deprived of the opportunity to make love themselves, a tyrannical instinct obliges them to do so vicariously.

Rarely did our disagreements with Antonietta reignite in the afternoon. Clara's benevolent influence seemed to prevail until the following morning. However, one had to take care with the words one used, something that's difficult for me in my old age. Gaffes really plague me as the years go by.

We were sitting on the verandah after supper, around the time when my drunkard and his song usually floated by. We had been chatting away, cheerfully, I dare say, in contrast to other evenings, although my good cheer was tied up in slightly sour complaints about my nephew Carlo, Guido's son—that evening, I was conscious of his defects—whom I accused of being not very affectionate and not very serious. Antonietta had agreed with me, and that made me more loquacious than usual. It was a great comfort to have my dear daughter backing me. I'm always so alone! It felt as if I were resting on her arm, or maybe her slight weight was resting on me.

I'd been distracted by a stroll along the path around the walls of the villa, in hopes I'd find my wino and be further cheered. But he didn't appear that evening. I smiled, thinking he had perhaps imbibed more than his usual portion and was now singing his sweet song flat on some bench in the park. True, he couldn't sing; but without music, he'd never be able to sleep.

It was late; time to turn in. But first I wanted to thank Antonietta for the lovely hours we'd spent. I kissed her forehead and whispered, "Thank you my dear. We've had a fine evening together."

But her face immediately darkened. For a moment she was silent, then speaking slowly as if plumbing her soul, said, "Yes, an evening just as if Valentino were not dead." Now she hesitated briefly, then burst into tears and ran off to her room. Augusta went after her, but the girl saw her and quickly shut herself in. Augusta stood in front of the door, quietly begging her to open it. Antonietta did nothing, and I, quite indignant, turned on my heel and headed off to my bed. I was not only indignant, but deeply offended. Good Lord! When a man is seventy, such a lack of respect doesn't escape his notice.

And my ire didn't subside for quite a while. I turned in but I could not sleep. Much later the thought came: Maybe I was the one in the wrong. Why had I needed to call attention to the fact that my loose talk about Carlo's character amused her? She suffered remorse when her thoughts wandered from the dead man and when she let go of her grief even for a few hours, and I knew it and nevertheless felt the need to warn her she was straying. It seemed that this descendant of mine had a weakness for total dedication, for taking vows. I saw myself in my daughter, twisted as she was, and not very lovable. It felt nightmarish. Now that my music was of better quality, because of the gramophone, I remembered that back when I first played the violin my notes had been approximate and my rhythms wrong: in short, something like Alfio's pictures. Was I not so different from Alfio and his pictures? I tossed and turned in bed, feeling remorseful.

When Augusta came to join me, I struggled to take control and rebel against this view, and the notion that I, although innocent, was probably the source of all the bestiality that poisoned my house. "What did she say?" I asked Augusta, pretending I was just waking up. It was meant as a proof of my utter innocence, that innocence so close to sleep.

She told me that Antonietta had said that when I praised our evening together, she had actually thought she heard a rebuke from the mouth of Valentino himself. And I fell back on the pillow, defeated. What a struggle! I had only meant to say that the evening had been so pleasant that I felt ready to fall asleep right away. Mine certainly wasn't the kind of joy that could deflate her mourning.

Augusta sighed and settled into her bed, moving the armchair where her little dog, well covered, was sleeping closer to her. "You know very well what she's like," she muttered.

I felt she blamed me for having made our daughter thus. I didn't say a word. I didn't protest that evening. I saw my life as a bundle of regrets and remorse, but quite honestly, I didn't think I had committed any crimes. Perhaps I had, but I couldn't remember any, nor could Antonietta, who'd gotten the less desirable part of the inheritance. There are those who inherit the father's long, crooked nose, while their siblings grow up tall and proud, or have his expressive eyes. She had inherited my remorse, and she found it quite unbearable because it made no sense to her.

Soon Augusta's breathing, which has grown louder over the years, told me she was already asleep. There in the dark, I stuck out my tongue at her, like a naughty child. Her naiveté seemed quite excessive to me. I'd been left all alone to suffer my remorse. The penance for having spoken out of turn was somewhat justified. But it was terribly cruel, intolerable, having to see my worst defects reborn in my children.

Carlo is such an amusing person that you can enjoy yourself just talking about him. He, too, seems not to have inherited anything from his father. Perhaps there is his self-assurance, Guido's self-assurance in playing the violin. I'm looking for the most unlikely analogy. Except that Carlo plays no instrument, and shows his self-assurance in knowing how to live and enjoy life. To live wisely, that is, and choose unerringly what will not damage him, and enjoy life to the fullest. At times he looks a bit tired, but beyond his health (which he neglects even though he's a medical student—does that perhaps raise questions about the validity of his studies?) nothing else is affected. From his parents he receives a modest monthly allowance that covers his needs perfectly. He's opposed to the appreciation of the lira, which isn't in his interest because he receives his allowance in foreign currency, but otherwise he takes no interest in politics. Maybe his new nationality has distanced him from our old homeland, but I don't think he bothers much about that. Now that he speaks Italian perfectly, I have the impression that his language is livelier than that of his peers. Most of us use words that have become somewhat withered from long use. Who makes an effort to be inventive? Carlo, however, cheerfully translates expressions from his Argentine Spanish into Italian, and everything he says sounds fresh without any effort at all. He studies whatever he wants. He even knows some snippets of Greek and Latin by heart, and recites them somewhat angrily, remembering the effort he put into learning them. He confessed to me himself that the reason he grew so thin back then was that he'd had to squeeze through the keyhole to pass Greek and Latin at gymnasium and *liceo*.

He's a devoted lover of women. No matter how much he enjoys games of all kinds (especially cards), he loudly insists that there is really only one kind of pleasure in this world. And he never stops alluding to that pleasure, allusions that, if they weren't always very witty, would be offensive. Sometimes he gets annoyed at Augusta, who never understands his double entendres. The two of us, naughty boys, laugh a lot, but never as much as when she finally does understand. When she finally does, she nearly falls off her chair laughing. When he's present, a lighthearted good cheer spreads through the gathering, unless of course serious obstacles are present, such as, in our household: an Alfio offended on account of his painting, or an Antonia in deep mourning.

His good cheer is never diminished by any worries. He tells us he has been hounded for days by bad luck at cards. "But misfortune is never due to bad cards," he says, as if this were a novel discovery. "At poker, it's the good hand that's responsible for real losses. Unfortunately, I've been lucky this week." He rarely loses, because he always knows how to play slightly better than his opponents. And he can play all the games. In recent years I learned about a difficult game called bridge. I learned about it at the very same time that I learned that the very best player of that game, who'd just arrived from England, was Carlo.

"Son of a bitch," I thought, forgetting that he was Guido's son. "He knows all the games. And he's even better than I am at the one card game I still play, a kind of solitaire that's not too complicated." I stopped playing any other card games years ago. Whenever I sat down at the card table, I'd immediately feel I was a condemned man, a feeling so pathetic I had to quit. It's strange! I feel so young and yet I'm utterly different from what I was as a young man. Can this be what genuine old age is?

Glancing at my cards, he warns me of a mistake I am making. Then he turns his attention away, to his newspaper, only to intervene again with a timely hint that really is helpful, in fact invaluable to me, sitting there with my eyes fixed on the cards. However, even though I don't let him see it, his involvement annoys me, upsets me: I love solitaire because it's solitary. But I also accept his hints because, as everybody knows, someone who's not in the game sees more clearly than the players, distracted by the very effort they're obliged to make.

I find his company extremely pleasant. Although I've long been in the care of Dr. Raulli, the purgative I take every day was prescribed by Carlo, and for a month now I've been using the expectorant he recommended (to tell the truth, it seemed like a miracle cure at first, but now less so). Finally, my diet, once again on his advice, is quite exacting. I've lost weight, and feel better now than I have for years, if truth be told. If I keep this up, who knows what feats I'll be accomplishing when I'm eighty. One merely has to give the diet time to take effect; it's slow-acting.

For all these reasons I'm very attached to him. When I am feeling morose, instead of feeding me cheering speeches, he'll touch my wrist, or perhaps make fun of me. His pale handsome face can look derisory while also showing affection. In any case, there's no cause to take offense, because a tiny note of derision is built into that face: his carefully shaved upper lip hangs down a bit, its slight swelling immediately visible among so many neat, precise lines.

And then there's something else that draws me to him. He's the first person in my life—in all my seventy years—that I've ever been able to be honest with. And honesty is marvelously relaxing, a great rest and repose after all my struggles. God only knows why I'm honest with him. It might just be a desire not to deceive my doctor. I've always been honest with Carlo, if not completely. He's intelligent, not indiscreet, and a slight hint from me is all he needs to understand. I never named Carla, nor any of the others, and he knows nothing of my conquests in the humbler quarters of town, he doesn't even suspect. He has a lot of fun with me, and I with him. He boasts of his adventures, and his boasts are so cheerful I can't help but enjoy them. Maybe I've been slightly dishonest, in that I exaggerate a bit. Not much, though, and not often. Only about the number of women. But I do exaggerate their attributes, yes. Although I never went so far as to boast of any princesses. There was one that I spoke of as a duchess so as not to confess she was the wife of a commendatore. I guess I could have said she was the wife of a cavaliere without being indiscreet, but I didn't. I wanted to appear important to Carlo, and besides, being honest made me feel so good that I imagined exaggerating I was being even more honest. Maybe it was a way of finding out what I might have done, if others had let me. A confession more honest than mere confession.

And Carlo was always very discreet.

He dined with us every Sunday. It was the best supper of the week for me. He was so firmly oblivious to the moods and whims of others that he never noticed when anyone was in bad spirits unless they complained loudly, and so he could laugh and enjoy himself even when sitting beside the inconsolable Antonietta. He didn't offend her; he didn't even notice her. And I tried to do the same, as far as I could. Of course I could never completely forget Antonietta's grief or Alfio's rancor the way he did. But it was easier for me when Cima was there. Together, we three were stronger against the gloomy two and poor Augusta's embarrassed silence; she didn't have the courage to rebel against her dear daughter in her presence, but she would later complain to me at length in private.

Now one evening we began talking about marital fidelity. The first name to emerge was Valentino's—a fact I couldn't understand because his fidelity was now absolute and permanent. Then Augusta had the bad taste of bringing *me* up, and she spoke about the matter at length until suddenly it dawned on Antonietta that her own faithful man was dead, and she began to grieve for that dead fidelity while lucky Augusta had a docile, sweet, and faithful husband who was still alive.

All of a sudden Carlo burst out laughing. It was a truly atrocious moment for me. He was laughing so hard he couldn't speak, and as my embarrassment stretched on I began to plan what I'd say in my defense. I would defend the happiness of my marriage tooth and nail, as I'd always done over the years. I'd find a way! I would say that I had lied to Carlo so that we could laugh about it. He was mistaken, deceived by me and me alone. That would persuade Augusta. But how would it go down with Alfio and Antonietta, younger and much less ingenuous?

When Carlo could speak again, he asked me, "How many years has it been since you were faithful?"

"I don't understand," I stammered. I didn't insist I was innocent, for I knew Carlo didn't mean recent adventures, of which there might not be any, and about which he certainly knew nothing. If he had asked, "How many years have you been faithful, Uncle?" I would have had a ready reply: "I've always been faithful! It's you who was duped, you're the one I fooled, you rascal."

"Well," Carlo went on, "Uncle's present state cannot be defined as fidelity. And I wanted to know for how many years he hasn't been faithful."

Now this was a sensitive point, but not as sensitive as he had seemed to mean to raise at first. I stuck my nose in my plate to hide my face, in case I looked uneasy. Then I laughed: "You, too, will one day find you are faithful perforce."

But Carlo—and here he amply demonstrated his discretion—said, "Yet in my case it will be called something else, because it won't come after self-imposed fidelity."

At this, I exhaled at last, but it had been such a terrible quarter of an hour that I decided that when Carlo finally returned to Buenos Aires I would give up the practice of honesty altogether, however difficult I might find it. Why open myself to such a risk for the mere love of chat, now that I didn't run other risks?

There had been talk he was having an affair with a married woman; this must have been what was keeping him in Trieste, because I don't suppose there was any dearth of people needing care in Buenos Aires. His mother had written, calling for him to return, but he pretended not to hear. He never neglected his mother, who lived for him alone, her only son now that his twin brother had died, and wrote her a brief postcard every day. But he didn't enjoy living with her. It seemed she tormented him with too much affection, and treated him like child who needed constant encouragement and advice. I thought those postcards, which must have arrived in Buenos Aires in large batches, were funny. Carlos, rueful, told me that was just how she was. She'd insisted he send them, checked that he wrote her each day, and would complain if he missed one. "I know," he'd sigh, "that I'll have to go back in the end.

"But then, there are women in Buenos Aires, too," he concluded.

Now I found the tendency of his mother, Ada, to exaggerate interesting, in fact it even made me feel relieved. However, it had nothing to do with me. Which meant the Malfenti family had played its part in the exaggeration that came out in my line.

One fine day I decided to prove it to Augusta. I had discovered for the first time what she thought of me. She told me, smiling meekly and affectionately. I reminded her of Alfio. Both physically and morally. Women are always poor at describing things precisely. She couldn't offer proof of what she felt. But she saw him, heard him, and above all loved him in a certain way, and she loved me in the same way. And then Antonietta also resembled me. Although she couldn't prove it. "But there's something similar about you two. Something I don't like, that I don't like in you in the same way, except that in you it arouses my compassion, it makes me feel sorry for you, you know, while in her, on the other hand, it makes me feel a bit angry."

We were in the car, heading toward the castle of Miramare. The sun had just set and it was blissful to look out upon the great expanse of water gleaming with pearly, serene colors that seemed in no way related to the blinding, brilliant reflections of before. I surrendered to this peacefulness, trying to ignore the kindhearted woman at my side, who understood me better than I—and, I hope, she—knew.

And for a moment I watched human traits being handed down one from the other, deformed from generation to generation yet transparently identical, so that even Augusta, without the benefit of reason, could recognize them. But then I drew back: What was the good of the law of heredity if anything could descend from anything? One might as well be ignorant of it if one had to accept Carlo had descended from that oaf Guido, and those two fools Antonietta and Alfio from me.

Carlo, however, already had something of a reputation as a young doctor in the city. He knew how to deal with everyone, protecting the dignity of those who mattered, indifferent where dignity was irrelevant, always looking after his own. Even Raulli admired him, but, I suspect, feared him a little too. It seemed that when he had first been given duties at the hospital, Carlo had voiced a rather unlikely diagnosis. Raulli, in front of the other doctors, called him ignorant. Carlo fought back, defending himself with a comment that circulated first among the medical men, then spread outside the hospital, creating such fame for him he might have brought some moribund patient back to life. Even today, when a Dr. Speyer's name is mentioned, people will laugh: "You mean the man of ignorance and error?"

That man was Carlo. He had told Raulli that, yes, ignorance was characteristic of young doctors, but as the history of medicine proved most definitively, all their elders were in error. Raulli, struck dumb and knowing he was in the wrong, managed to croak out a reply: "That was true until half a century ago, young man, but not any longer."

And now someone claims to find a resemblance to Guido in Carlo. Guido, high-handed as long as he is in a position to hurt, cowardly and speechless as soon as he feels under threat.

Now this magnificent doctor's nose for business—and this was the quality in him that I found so seductive—might well have been inherited from his grandfather Giovanni Malfenti. However, I do know that my father-in-law's talent for business developed quite late in life, along with his large belly. And it was hard to see how that talent could have come down to someone so light and graceful as Carlo, when Giovanni's business sense seemed part and parcel of his great girth, part of the meditative state that left him so sedate and serene.

Carlo, on the other hand, was alert and somewhat nervous—and therefore quite lively. When he sat beside you, you felt he was real company, a substantial presence. He was never still, often tapping a heel rapidly on the floor. The "heel roll," he'd announce, smiling, as if he couldn't help it. He smokes with great, great pleasure, very fine cigarettes. While Alfio, who also smokes, goes at it furiously with those stinking Tuscan cigars of his. He hasn't even inherited the smoking from me.

My great affection for Carlo is partly due, certainly, to how alone my two children leave me feeling. The proof of that is the fact that Augusta, who is much more needful of affection than I, also sought a Carlo among her court of animals, and when they did not suffice, took on Renata, now her inseparable companion.

Renata began working for Antonietta four years ago, replacing Umbertino's old wet nurse, who moved back to her village. She came to us when Antonietta moved in and then, when Umbertino did not need looking after because he had started school, she transferred into Augusta's service. Renata continued to keep the boy company in the evening, though, because he could not fall asleep by himself in that night populated by so many aggressive beasts, and Antonietta spent her evenings with us after dinner.

And so Renata has an easy, but somewhat complicated, life. She doesn't have much to do (at present she merely cleans the dining room, the sitting room, and my study), but the easy life ties her up all day long. She cuts the bread that's put out on the terrace every day for the sparrows, keeps the two canary cages in order, and looks after the care and amusement of Musette. All this apparently entertains her no end, because she's forever in good spirits, and it's so pleasant to be served by people who are smiling. You have all the convenience without suffering any remorse! On the way to my study I have to pass by the kitchen, and I never fail to hear the husky sound of Renata's frank and abundant laugh bubbling up.

Just as it was easy for me to join Augusta in loving her animals, it was easy for me to imitate her love for Renata. Paternal love, of course, considering how old I am. But I do love to see her, young thing that she is, figure so nicely turned, her small body atop legs that are rather long, slim, and nervous. Her head isn't quite perfect, but it's very graceful, with dark-brown curls, sparkling eyes, and beautiful teeth. She comes from Friuli, and she takes a fifteen-day leave every year to visit her mother, although she always comes back looking slightly undernourished.

One day Augusta wanted to see how her Renata was treated, and so we drove out to her village close to Gorizia in our car. She was warned of our arrival and was waiting for us on the main road, neat and clean. Blushing, she said she'd come out to meet us because her house stood on a narrow alleyway too small for cars.

But Augusta insisted. "Oh, but I wanted to meet your mother."

"There she is," said Renata, who had turned red, red with that laugh of hers that was slightly fractured.

At a signal from Renata, an old woman sitting alone on a bench under a huge horse chestnut rose and came over to us. She was dressed in her best, in very old-fashioned garb, long skirts and a colored kerchief knotted elegantly around her head. Everything, however—including the gray and toothless woman herself—was faded, colorless. She insisted on kissing Augusta's hand. She spoke almost perfect Friulan, and neither Augusta nor I could understand even one of the rough sounds issuing from that mouth without the necessary organs to regulate them, first from the right-hand side, then from the left.

Then our chauffeur Fortunato spoke up, and things relaxed somewhat. He himself was a native of that place, and when he began to speak in Friulan the old lady's jaw just about fell off from laughing. She was bent in two with mirth, perhaps exaggerating to conceal her embarrassment. Augusta presented the gifts she had brought, and Renata encouraged her mother to return home, where her brother would soon be returning from work, needing his supper. The old woman insisted that his food was already prepared and had been since morning, before she left, following her daughter's instructions.

"Trust me." Fortunato broke out in a smile. "Polenta can always wait. It's the most patient supper in the world."

In short, we understood that Renata did not want us to visit her house, and we had to leave without seeing it.

I asked Fortunato how he had become acquainted with Renata's mother. The scoundrel explained to me that the people of those villages knew each other as well as if they all lived in the same quarter of the city. Soon afterward, we discovered that he and Renata were bedding down together.

In the beginning, this troubled us. It seemed to diminish Renata's dignity. Fortunato had only recently become our driver, after a magnificent horse called Hydran had turned broken-winded only two years after his purchase, a horse we had sadly run into the ground wishing to treat him as normal. Then, quite distressed about his death, we didn't want to have anything more to do with horses, and because we had loved this one so much we refused all contact with the species—so patient with man until man, impatient himself, did not return the favor.

And so Fortunato the coachman, following a long series of lessons that left me for months without either carriage or motorcar, rose to the dignified office of chauffeur. He was slow to learn, but once he had, he never forgot. At first he was unable get up the speed to arrive at our destination, but now he drives quite fast, sometimes too fast, and after every longish expedition I'm plagued with speeding fines from all over. Fortunato insists it's impossible to please the guards, for whom it seems the fines are part and parcel of their income. And this may well be true. Fortunato the chauffeur, surprised and indignant, reacts to certain breakdowns with helpless fury. His coachman's soul suggests he apply the whip. Once we had to leave him and the car out in the countryside, luckily not terribly far from town, and return home on foot. He came back late at night, and, so I'm told, cursing. He had forgotten to look at the fuel gauge, and it was late, far too late when he noticed that the tank was dry. It's true that ever after when the car came to a halt, his eye would automatically dash to the fuel gauge. He never learned except from breakdowns, and I couldn't take it anymore. "We old people," said Augusta fatalistically, "don't like seeing new faces."

And so Fortunato stayed home. He also does gardening duties, not very capably, but with a certain feeling. He doesn't have much to do. Which was how he found the time to seduce our young friend. She treated him as if he was already her husband, that is, without great affection. She liked to call him the Breakdown Man, at which I laughed wickedly once Carlo had shown me how to enjoy it. They also had some quarrels over work. She thought he should be responsible for keeping order in the drawing room, because there were plants in there, and when he protested, she just laughed. "But isn't all that is mine, yours?"

He was much slower than she—a quick girl who understood your meaning before you finished talking. It's true that Renata then often forgot things, while Fortunato never did, once he had made you waste a huge amount of breath before grasping exactly what you were saying to him.

It was also curious how on the way to understanding, he would take an interest in details of no concern to him. For example he might be charged with giving a message to Augusta when he went to fetch her at the house of one of her friends. "All right, then," he'd repeat, "I must be at the Guggenheims' door at six p.m. and when Signora Augusta comes down..." He would make a detailed analysis of everyone's movements. And I, impatient, would shout, "Allow the signora to come down the stairs alone!" He'd then shake himself all over as if he were about to lose his balance, and I would understand that I had to let him say as many words as he needed to keep his thoughts in order.

In the evening, when Augusta and I were turning in, I'd say to her, "How can that child live with a man so unintelligent?"

And Augusta: "Well, I don't think one needs intelligence to be happy."

Poor Fortunato, however, was running a real risk. We had decided to keep our little housemaid as close to us as possible. I suggested an extra room that would be useful for the children that might arrive. But one evening Augusta told me they had decided not to have children, although they would accept the extra room for a gramophone—which wailed only on demand.

A few evenings later she told me that our little minx Renata had confided that if she'd felt the need to have children, she would have had the job done by someone sharper than Fortunato.

We laughed at that, Augusta and I. She, because she thought Renata's words were teasing and inconsequential, and I because that "sharper" really pleased me and I didn't care whether she'd meant it seriously or not. So Renata, too, was pondering the laws of heredity?

But Carlo (to whom I usually related most everything, to see how the present generation reacts to matters about which I might be out of my depth) told me, "No, you're mistaken, Uncle. She isn't thinking about heredity at all. Her mind's on what she needs right now."

I didn't understand just then, but I pretended to laugh, and when I did understand I laughed out loud. Then, reflecting on it, I decided that maybe Carlo had it right, but at the same time, maybe I did too. What are the needs of the present? Are they not dictated by some imperious design that is preparing the future?

MY LEISURE

ONE CAN'T look for the present on a calendar or clock, instruments useful only to mark a personal relationship with the past or to move into the future with some semblance of preparation. The present—the real present—is composed of oneself and the things and people that surround one.

My own present is actually told in various tenses. A first, lengthy present begins with my withdrawal from business. It began eight years ago. A heartrending example of inertia. Although there are some highly significant events that divide it. For instance, my daughter's marriage, an event well in the past which figures in the other lengthy present, interrupted—or maybe refreshed, or better, corrected—by the death of her husband. There's the birth of my grandson, Umberto, also distant, because the true present where Umberto is concerned is my affection for him, a conquest he's not even aware he made, which he imagines is his birthright. Does he believe in anything, that miniature soul? His, and my, present as it relates to him, are those sure, small steps of his interrupted by bitterly painful fears, in turn soothed by his army of dollies when he can't win the aid of his mother, or his grandfather, me. My present is also Augusta as she is today—poor thing!—with her animals, her dogs, cats, and birds, and the perpetual indisposition of which she refuses to cure herself properly. She does the minimum that Dr. Raulli prescribes, and won't listen either to me—who, making a superhuman effort, overcame the same tendency to heart fatigue—or to Carlo (Guido's son, our nephew), who's just back from university and knows all the most modern medicines.

It must be said that a large part of my present comes from the pharmacy. I can't recall exactly when this present began, but it was a period thoroughly defined by new medicines and new ideas. Whatever happened to those days when I thought I was providing for all my organism's needs by swallowing a hefty dose of compound licorice powder every evening, or one of those simple powdered or liquid bromides? Today, with Carlo's help, I have far different means at my disposal to fight disease. Carlo tells me everything he knows, and I, on the other hand, don't say everything I imagine, because I fear he won't agree with me, and will destroy with his objections the castle I have struggled to build, which ensures me a peace of mind and security that people of my age don't usually enjoy. A real castle! Carlo believes I accept his every suggestion so promptly because I have faith in him. Anything but! I know he's very knowledgeable, and I try to learn from him and follow, but with discretion. My arteries are in a sorry state, no doubt about that. Last summer my blood pressure shot up to 240 mm. Whether on account of the pressure or not, I was very, very low at the time. But large doses of iodide (or some other medicine whose name I can never remember) brought my pressure to 160, where it has remained since . . . here I stop writing for a moment to measure it on the device that sits ready on my table. And it's just 160! I used to feel threatened by an apoplectic stroke that I was sure I could feel coming. And proximity to death didn't really make me a better person, because I despised all those who didn't feel threatened by a stroke, who looked unpleasantly like good people who sympathize, feel for others, and enjoy themselves.

Now, guided by Carlo, I treated even those organs of mine that had never in any way asked for help. Of course, every one of them was probably tired after so many years of work and could benefit from assistance. I gave them aid unasked. So often, when a person falls ill, the doctor sighs, "But you've called me too late." So much better to think ahead. I have no wish to undertake a cure for my liver when it shows no signs of illness, but I also don't want to expose myself to the fate of my friend's son: the picture of health at thirty-two years old, he had a violent attack of jaundice one day, turned yellow as a squash, and in forty-eight hours lay dead. "He'd never been sick," his poor father said. "Strong as an ox—and he had to die!" Many oxen do come to a bad end. It's something I've observed, and I'm quite happy not to be one of them. Caution never hurts, and so every Monday I send my liver a pill that protects it from sudden acute illnesses until the following Monday. I watch over my kidneys with regular analyses, and so far they've never shown signs of trouble. I know, however, that one day they may need assistance. The all-milk diet I follow on Tuesdays protects me somewhat for the rest of the week. It would be rich, however, if other people who never give their kidneys a thought were to enjoy their perfect functioning, while I, who every week make them a sacrifice, should suddenly be repaid with the nasty surprise that struck poor Copler.

Some five years ago I fell ill with chronic bronchitis. It prevented me from sleeping, and at times I was obliged to leap out of bed at night and spend hours sitting up in a chair. The doctor didn't say so, but I'm certain that heart fatigue was also involved. Raulli's prescription was to stop smoking, to slim, and to eat very little meat. To quit smoking was difficult, and so I sought to satisfy the prescription by doing without meat altogether. Slimming, too, was not at all that easy. At the time I weighed ninety-four kilograms net. In three years I lost two kilos, meaning that to arrive at the weight Raulli desired would have cost me another eighteen years. It is so difficult to eat little when one is abstaining from meat.

My slimming, I must confess, I owe to Carlo. It was one of his first medical successes. He suggested I skip one of my three daily meals, and I decided to sacrifice the supper that we in Trieste take at 8 p.m.—unlike other Italians, who have lunch at noon and dinner at seven. Every day I fasted for eighteen hours straight.

To begin with, I slept better. My heart, freed of the labor of digestion, could dedicate its every beat to bathing the veins, removing detritus from my organism, nourishing the lungs. I had known terrible insomnia, that great agitation that someone longing for peace feels just because he can't achieve it, and now I lay there quietly, calmly awaiting my just measure of warmth and repose, genuine respite in a wearying routine. Sleep after a splendid meal is quite another thing: the heart is wholly occupied with digestion and can't undertake any other duties.

All this taught me that I was more suited to abstinence than to moderation. It was easier not to eat supper at all than to have to hold back at breakfast and luncheon. There were no other limitations. Twice a day I could eat whatever I wanted. And that caused no harm because it was followed by eighteen hours of autophagy. At first, I followed up my midday meal of pasta and salad with a couple of eggs. Then I did away with those, too, not at Raulli's or Carlo's suggestion but following the sensible advice of a philosopher, Herbert Spencer, who put forth the law according to which organs that grow too quickly, because overnourished, are not as strong as those that grow more slowly. The law referred to children, of course, but I'm convinced that rotation is beneficial, and even a child of seventy does well to love his organs rather than overfeed them. Carlo agrees with my theory, and sometimes he even pretends to have invented it.

My efforts to do without supper were greatly aided by smoking, and for the first time in my life I was reconciled to my habit, even in theory. Smokers fast better than other people. A good smoke puts any appetite to sleep. It's to smoking that I owe the credit for having reduced my bodily weight to eighty kilos net. What peace of mind to be able to smoke for hygienic purposes! You can smoke a bit more than you should with a perfectly clear conscience. Health, it turns out, is a truly miraculous condition. Various organs must cooperate to achieve it, organs whose functions we know but never fully understand (as Carlo himself, who has studied all the science, even that of our ignorance, admits), so that it seems quite possible that perfect health does not exist. Otherwise the miracle would be that it can deteriorate. Things that move should be able to move for eternity. Isn't this the law of the heavens? And surely the relevant law applies on earth too. But as we know, disease is predestined from birth. From the very beginning, some organs are weaker and require a certain amount of effort to function, obliging one of the fraternal organs to work harder, and where there is effort, there is fatigue, and even, finally, death.

And thus, and only for that reason, illness followed by death is not a mark of any error in our design. I'm too ignorant to know whether death and reproduction take place up there in the heavens as they do down here on earth. All I know is that some stars and some planets exhibit imperfect trajectories. And, well, any planet that doesn't rotate on its axis is surely lame, blind, or hunchbacked.

Among our organs, one is at the center, almost like the sun in a solar system. Only a few years ago, this was thought to be the heart. But at present, as everyone knows, the sexual organ determines all. Even Carlo, who turns up his nose at those rejuvenation operations, will tip his hat to the sexual organs. He says that if we could succeed in rejuvenating the sexual organs, the whole organism would surely be rejuvenated. There was no need to tell me this. I had worked it out for myself. But they'll never succeed. God knows what effect the monkey gland will have. Will the patient, seeing a beautiful woman, feel inclined to climb the nearest tree? That, too, is juvenile behavior, I might add.

Let's face it, Mother Nature is maniacal: she has a mania for reproduction. She'll keep an organism alive so long as there's hope it will reproduce. Then she kills it, in many and varied ways, because her other mania is to remain mysterious. She wouldn't want to reveal herself by always employing the same ailment to suppress the old: some disease that makes it clear we're about to die, a small tumor always located in the same place.

I've always been an enterprising sort. Having decided against the operation, I nonetheless wanted to trick Mother Nature and make her think I was still fit for reproduction, so I found myself a mistress. It was the most tranquil affair I've ever had in my life. I didn't consider it a transgression, or a betrayal of Augusta. That would have been peculiar: to my mind, acquiring a mistress felt like a decision akin to entering a pharmacy.

But then of course the matter grew slightly more complicated. In time, it came to me that a person cannot be taken like a medicine. A person is a complex remedy containing a fairly large percentage of poison. I wasn't yet very aged. It happened three years ago, and I was therefore sixty-seven: not yet a very old man. And so my heart, which as an organ of secondary importance in the adventure was not supposed to interfere, ended up getting involved. And even Augusta profited at times from my adventure, and was loved, cherished, and rewarded as during the days of Carla. Strangely enough, she didn't find this surprising, or even notice the novelty. She inhabits a sphere of great calm, and finds it natural that I should pay less attention to her than in the past, and our present state of inertia hasn't weakened our ties, which bind us together with caresses and affectionate words. And those caresses and words don't need to be repeated for that strong and intimate tie between us to remain alive in some place. One day, when to soothe my conscience I propped two fingers under her chin and gazed into her faithful eyes at length, she melted, offering her lips to me, and said, "You have always been so loving." At the time I was somewhat surprised by that remark, but then, examining the past attentively I realize that I had never withheld affection or abjured my old love for her. I even took her in my arms somewhat absentmindedly every night before falling asleep.

It was really rather difficult to find the woman I was looking for. There was no one at home suited to the office, and anyway I was reluctant to sully my own household. I would have done so nonetheless—given my urgent need to trick Mother Nature so that she didn't think the hour had come for my fatal ailment, not to mention the huge problem of finding outside the household what I, an old man who dealt in economic affairs, needed. The most beautiful woman in the house was in fact Augusta. There was a girl of fourteen she employed for certain duties. But I knew if I approached the latter, Mother Nature, disapproving, would quickly exterminate me with that thunderbolt she always has in hand.

There's not much point in telling you how I found Felicita. In my passion for hygiene, I used to go every day to a stall well past Piazza Unità to supply myself with cigarettes, necessitating a walk of more than half an hour. The clerk was an older woman but the owner of the concession, who spent a few hours there every day keeping an eye, was Felicita herself, a young woman of about twenty-four. At first I thought she had inherited the tobacco concession, but later I learned she had purchased it with money of her own. I met her there. We soon came to an understanding. I liked her. A blond, she wore highly colorful clothes, of fabrics that weren't very costly but always new and quite flamboyant. She was vain about her beauty: her pretty, small head graced with hair cut short and thick with curls, her charming figure, held quite erect, as if supported by a pin, indeed, leaning slightly backwards. I sensed immediately that she liked colors. Her taste for bright hues was especially evident when she was at home. Sometimes the house wasn't well heated, and once I made note of the colors she was wearing: a red kerchief knotted around her head in the style our peasants wear; a yellow brocade scarf thrown over her shoulders, a quilted apron of red, yellow, and green over a blue skirt, and a pair of particolored embroidered wool slippers. She looked like a dainty oriental doll, but her small, pale face belonged firmly to our people, her eyes weighing people and things attentively to get what advantage she could. We quickly agreed on a monthly allowance: to tell the truth, so extravagant a sum that I could only regret the more sober prewar standards. When the twentieth of the month arrived, dear Felicita had already begun to speak of her stipend soon to fall due, so that the better part of the month was taken up with these calculations. She was perfectly frank and transparent; I, less so; she never knew that I had been propelled into her arms by reading medical texts.

I soon forgot that too. I must admit that today I do miss that house, so simple apart from a single room decorated in good taste and finery that measured up to what I was paying, the colors restrained and the light low, so that Felicita looked like a rare flower. She had a brother who lived in the same house; he was a competent electrical technician, a serious worker who earned a rather good day's wage. He looked somewhat emaciated, but it was quite apparent that this wasn't the reason he hadn't married; he hadn't married because he was careful with his money. When Felicita called him in to review the safety of the wiring in our room, I had occasion to talk to him. I learned that brother and sister were business partners hoping to accumulate a tidy sum in as short a time as possible. Felicita's life, between the stall and her home, was quite unfrivolous, and Gastone, between the repair shop and home, lived equally frugally. She must have earned quite a bit more than he did, but she didn't mind because for her—I would later learn—the assistance of her brother was essential. It was he who had obtained the tobacco concession that was proving such a good investment. He was so certain his way of life was superior, that when he spoke of other working men who spent all their earnings without a thought for the morrow he couldn't conceal his contempt.

I mean, we got along pretty well. Her tasteful, tidy, well-appointed room looked a little like a doctor's office. Only Felicita was a rather acid remedy, best to get down quickly, before the taste buds know what's what. Right away, in fact even before I'd agreed to our con-tract—to encourage my agreement—she'd put her arm around me and whispered, "I swear I don't find you repulsive." The effect was rather charming, for she said it very sweetly, but I was stunned nev-ertheless. Actually, it had never occurred to me that I wasn't repulsive. I rather thought this was love again, from which I'd long abstained out of a mistaken understanding of the rules of hygiene, so as to offer myself to someone who really desired me. This romantic notion was the hygiene I sought to practice, in the belief that any other kind of love would be partial and inadequate. Despite the sums the cure was costing me, however, I didn't have the courage to tell Felicita the person I wanted her to be. And she, utterly frank with me, often spoiled the mood quite ingenuously: "How odd! I don't find you repulsive." One day, employing all the brutality I'm sometimes ca-pable of, I murmured softly in her ear, "How odd! I don't find you repulsive either." That made her laugh so hard that the cure was inter-rupted.

And yet there are times when I go so far as to flatter myself—to show off, feel more confident, worthier, taller; to forget that I've dedicated a part of my life to not being repulsive—that Felicita really did love me in a few brief moments of our long affair. And trying to recall a genuine expression of her affection, it's not the invariable sweetness with which she always received me that I remember, or the maternal care with which she protected me from drafts of air, or her solicitude, one day when we were together and a storm blew up, and she covered me with her brother's overcoat and lent me an umbrella. What I recall instead is her sincerity that time she babbled, "Oh, you're so repulsive. You disgust me."

Talking with Carlo about medicine as usual one day, he said to me, "You need a girl who's a gerontophile."

He may be right. I didn't tell Carlo that perhaps I had found that girl once, and then lost her. Except that I don't think Felicita was a genuine gerontophile. She expected too much money for me to believe she loved me just as I was.

She was certainly the most expensive woman I have known in my entire life. She would coolly observe, those pretty, placid eyes of hers half closed to scrutinize better, how far I'd go in allowing myself to be sacked and pillaged. At first, and for a long time, she made do with the precise amount of her allowance, because I, not yet enslaved to her by force of habit, had said I wouldn't pay her more. She several times tried to put a hand in my pocket, but then stepped back so as not to risk losing me. One time, she succeeded. I gave her the money for a fairly costly fur, which I never actually saw. Another time she got me to bankroll an extravagant outfit from Paris, which she later showed off to me. Well, I may be blind, but her multicolored outfits are unforgettable, and I remembered I'd already seen her wearing that one. She was quite thrifty and would merely pretend to be capricious because she thought men were more likely to accept caprice in a woman than frugality or penny-pinching. And that is how, against my wishes, our affair came to an end.

Our arrangement was that I could visit her at certain hours two times a week. One Tuesday, having started out for her house, I got halfway there and decided I would rather be alone. I went back to my study and spent a peaceful afternoon with Beethoven's Ninth Symphony on the gramophone.

On Wednesday I still wasn't feeling a great urge for Felicita, but my avarice propelled me to her. I was paying her a hefty monthly allowance, and if I didn't take advantage of my rights, it was definitely costing me too much. I should also point out that when I take a cure, I'm very conscientious about applying it precisely, scientifically. Only then can be it be judged whether the cure was a bad or a good one.

So with all the speed my legs would permit, I arrived at what I considered *our* room. Which for the moment belonged to others. Big Misceli, a fellow of about my age, was sitting in an overstuffed chair in a corner while Felicita lay in great abandon on the sofa, enjoying a long, fine cigarette of a kind not supplied at her stall. It was, in truth, the very same tableau in which Felicita and I were to be found when we were alone, the only difference being that Misceli didn't smoke, while I joined Felicita in the pleasure.

"Is there some way I can be of help, sir?" inquired Felicita gelidly, studying with great interest the fingernails of the hand holding the cigarette.

I couldn't say a word. But presently I found it easier to speak because, in truth, I realized that I didn't resent Misceli at all. That corpulent fellow, about my age, who looked considerably older than I and was embarrassed that he weighed so much, gazed at me hesitantly over the gleaming spectacles poised on the tip of his nose. I always think that other old men are older than I am.

"Oh, Misceli," I said, determined not to make a scene, "what a long time since we've seen one another." And I held out my hand, and he placed his big paw in it, without moving it at all. He still didn't speak. He truly appeared older than me.

By this time, with all the objectivity of the man of good sense, I'd understood perfectly that my position was identical to that of Misceli. And therefore I concluded that there was no cause for resentment. After all, ours was merely a chance collision on the sidewalk. You just plow on, mumbling "Sorry," no matter how painful it may be for the presumed injured party.

This thought resurrected in me the gentleman I'd always been. I felt it behooved me to make things easier for Felicita too. So I said to her, "My good signorina, I need a hundred packets of Sport cigarettes, chosen with some care, because I am giving them as a present. Fresh ones, mind you. Your stall is a bit out of the way, so I took the liberty of coming up for a moment."

Felicita stopped looking at her nails and turned very gracious. She rose, and even walked me to the door. In a low voice tarred with reproach, she hissed, "Why didn't you come yesterday?" Then immediately, "And why today?"

I was offended. It seemed appalling that my visits were limited to fixed days—and at the price I was paying. I settled for the comfort of venting my rage. "I've only come to inform you that I'm done with you and that we will not see each other again!"

She gazed at me in surprise, and in order to see me better, stepped back from me, leaning for a moment even farther back. It was a strange posture, but it lent her a certain grace: she looked sure of herself and able to keep her balance in difficult circumstances.

"As you wish," she said with a shrug. But then, perhaps to be certain she'd heard me right, she asked, hand on the door, searching my face, "So we're not to see each other again?"

"That's right. Never again," I said, slightly annoyed. I was starting down the stairs when big Misceli noisily came to the door, shouting, "Wait, hold on. I'm coming with you. I just had to tell the signorina how many packets of Sport I need. One hundred. Like you." Down the stairs we went together, while Felicita slowly closed the door—hesitating at length, which flattered me.

We took the long slope that leads down to Piazza Unità slowly, watching where we put our feet. Working our way downhill, Misceli, the heavier of us two, certainly looked older than me. Once he even tripped and almost fell, and I readily came to his aid. He didn't thank me. He was breathing heavily and we hadn't even finished struggling down that slope. That, and that alone, explains why he was silent. And in fact, when we got down to the flats behind city hall, he began to gush, "I personally don't smoke Sports. But they're the cigarettes the people prefer. I need a present for a carpenter who works for me, and I wanted to get him some good ones. And Signorina Felicita knows how to find them." Now that he was talking, he could proceed only one step at a time. When he had to rummage in a trouser pocket, he came to a complete halt. Out came a gold cigarette case; he pressed a little button and it sprang open. "Would you like one?" he asked. "Nicotine-free." I said yes, and I, too, stopped, to light it. He hadn't moved while struggling to return the case to his pocket. I thought, "She might have given me a worthier rival." The truth was, I was steadier than he was both on the slope and on the flats. Compared to him, I was not much more than a lad. He even smoked tasteless nicotine-free cigarettes. I was so much more manly: though I'd tried to quit smoking countless times, I'd never been tempted by those tomfool nicotine-free cigarettes.

God was willing, and so we arrived at the gates of the Tergesteo, where our paths would diverge. By now Misceli had moved on to quite different topics: stock market affairs about which he seemingly knew a great deal. He looked hot and somewhat distracted. As if, when he talked, he never listened to what he was saying. Like me, who also didn't listen, but only stared at him, trying to determine what he wasn't saying.

I didn't want to leave him without making an effort to learn what was going on in his mind. To that end, I began unburdening myself. "That Felicita is a real trollop," I spat out. Now Misceli offered a fresh spectacle: embarrassment. His large lower jaw began sawing away like a ruminant's. Maybe he would work up to speaking by moving that part of him until he decided what he wanted to say?

He replied, "Not in my view. She offers excellent Sports." Was he going to carry on with this silly comedy forever? Annoyed, I shot back, "Really now, you would go back to visit Signorina Felicita again?"

Another moment of hesitation. His jawbone jutted forward, traveled left, then right, and finally came to rest in its proper place. Then, for the first time betraying an urge to laugh, he said, "Of course, I'll visit her again when I'm in need of more of those Sports."

I laughed too. But I wanted to know more. "So why then did you leave today?"

He paused again, and in his dusky eyes, fixed on something down

at the end of the road, I thought I saw great sadness. "Well, I'm su-
perstitious. Whenever I am interrupted in the midst of something,
I immediately think I see the hand of Providence, and I quit what
I'm doing. Once when I was about to go to Berlin on some important
business, I abandoned the trip at Sesana where the train, for some
reason, was stalled for several hours. I believe the affairs of this world
must not be forced—especially not at our age."

That still wasn't enough for me, and I asked, "It didn't bother you
that I, too, was visiting Signorina Felicita for the Sports?"

A quick and decisive reply left his jaw no time to rotate. "I should
care? You think I'm jealous? We may be permitted to make love from
time to time. But not to be jealous, because jealousy too easily exposes
a man to ridicule. Never jealous! If you want my advice, don't ever
let anyone see you jealous; they'll laugh at you."

Good-natured as his words sound on paper, his tone was fairly sharp,
and acid with irony and contempt. His large face reddened as he drew
close to me; he was shorter than I, and looking upward as if to determine where on my body was the most vulnerable point to strike. Why
was he so angry at me, even though he insisted he was not jealous?
What else had I done to him? Could it be that he was angry at me
because I'd held up his train at Sesana, when he was planning to arrive in Berlin?

I wasn't jealous either. That is, I'd have liked to know how much
he paid Felicita monthly. I felt that if I were to learn that he paid
her—as seemed perfectly right to me—more than I did, I would be
quite content.

But I didn't have time even to begin investigating. All of a sudden,
Misceli grew meek and called on my discretion. His mild-mannered
air turned threatening, however, when he recalled that we were in
the same boat. I reassured him: I too was married and knew what
trouble an incautious word could bring in our circumstances.

"Oh, but it's not for my wife that I counsel discretion," he said,
waving a hand soothingly. "My wife hasn't troubled herself about

certain things for many years. And I know that you too are in Dr. Raulli's care. Now he's threatening not to see me anymore if I don't follow his prescriptions: if I drink even one glass of wine, if I smoke more than ten cigarettes a day, the nicotine-free ones, mind you, and don't abstain from...all the rest. He says the body of a man of our age only stays upright in equilibrium, because it can't decide which way to collapse. Therefore one mustn't even hint at any particular direction, or the decision will be soon made. You know," he said, sounding sorry for himself, "it's easy to prescribe for someone else: don't do this, or that, or that other thing. You might as well advise him to accept dying a few months sooner, rather than go on living like that."

He lingered for a moment, inquiring about my health. I told him my blood pressure had once shot up to 240 mm, a fact that pleased him greatly because his had only risen as high as 220. One foot on the stairs leading up to the Tergesteo, he bid me a friendly farewell, cautioning, "Lips sealed, please."

Raulli's excellent rhetorical figure—the elderly body that stays on its feet because it doesn't know which way it should fall—obsessed me for several days. The old doctor, when he spoke of "where" or "in what direction," clearly meant which *organ* would give way. And that concept of *equilibrium* also meant something specific. Raulli knew what he was talking about. For the old, "health" is a progressive and simultaneous weakening of all the organs. It's a problem if one of them lags behind, remaining too young. Then, I suppose, the cooperation among them turns to conflict, and the weak organs take a pummeling—with what magnificent consequences for the overall system you can imagine. So perhaps Misceli's appearance was an act of Providence, guarding my life, even sending word to me by means of that roving-jawed mouth about how I was to behave.

I returned, thoughtful, to my gramophone. In the Ninth Symphony I rediscovered the organs, cooperating and in conflict. Cooperating in the first movements, especially the scherzo where even the kettledrums are permitted to sum up with their two notes what the other instruments around them are murmuring. While the joy of the final movement sounded like rebellion to my ears. Crude, with all the force of violence, interrupted by modest, short-lived regrets and hesitations. Not for nothing does the human voice, the least reasonable-sounding thing in all of nature, appear in the last movement. Yes, other times I'd interpreted that symphony differently, as a most powerful expression of harmony between battling forces, into which the human voice enters and merges. But that day the same symphony played on the same records sounded different.

"Farewell, Felicita," I murmured when the music died out. I mustn't give her any more thought. She wasn't worth risking a sudden collapse. There are so many medical theories in this world that it is hard to know which to submit to. Those no-account doctors only make life more difficult. Even the simplest things are quite complicated. To abstain from alcohol is evidently a wise prescription. At the same time it's known that sometimes alcohol has curative properties. Must I therefore wait until the doctor orders it before permitting myself the comfort of that potent medication?

It's well known that death can at times result from an organ's sudden caprice, possibly only transitory, or from a passing chance coincidence of several deficiencies. I mean, something that might have been a momentary disorder, had it not been followed by death. And it's up to us to make sure it remains momentary. The action to be taken must be prompt and perhaps preempt the cramp due to overexertion or the collapse from inertia. What point is there in waiting for the doctor, who comes and hastens to make out his bill? I alone am warned in time, by a slight upset, of the need for assistance. Unfortunately the doctors don't know how to be of aid in such cases. I therefore swallow various things: I knock back a purgative with a sip of wine, and then observe myself. Perhaps I need something else: a glass of milk, and along with it a few drops of digitalis. In the minuscule quantities the distinguished Hahnemann advised. The mere presence of those tiny quantities are sufficient to produce the reactions that foster life, as if an organ, more than needing to be fed or stimulated, needs to be reminded. It sees a drop of calcium and declares, "Oh look. I had forgotten. I'm supposed to be working."

This was why Felicita was deadly. You couldn't dose her.

That evening Felicita's brother came to see me. When he appeared I was so overwhelmed with alarm that Augusta herself had to show him the way to my study. Dreading what he might have to say to me, I was quite happy when Augusta quickly left us alone. He undid the knot of a handkerchief from which he took a package. One hundred packs of Sport cigarettes: he divided them into five lots of twenty, and so it was easy to verify the count. He then showed me that each pack was soft to the touch. They had been selected one by one from a large shipment. He was sure I'd be satisfied.

And in fact I was very satisfied indeed, because after having been so frightened, I now felt completely reassured. I immediately paid him the 160 lire I owed and even cheerfully thanked him. Cheerfully: I was seized by a strong desire to laugh. What an odd woman, Felicita. You could abandon her, but she wouldn't fail to look after her business.

But when this tall, spindly, pallid fellow had stuffed his pocket with the money received, he made no move to leave. Actually, he didn't look like Felicita's brother. I'd seen him on other occasions, but always better dressed. He wore no collar and his clothing, although clean enough, was quite threadbare. Oddly, he was wearing a special hat on a work day, but it was absolutely filthy and badly deformed from long use.

He was staring hard at me, hesitating to speak. His slightly sullen expression seemed to gleam with misplaced light, as if to will me to guess what he had in mind. When he finally began to speak, he looked imploring, so imploring that I couldn't help but feel it was a threat. Fervent begging can come very close to threatening. In the hands of some peasants, the same holy cards they devote their prayers to end up, punished, under their beds.

At last, in a confident voice, he said, "Felicita says it's the tenth of the month."

I looked at the calendar, from which I daily tear off a page. "She's quite right. It's the tenth today, no doubt about it."

"Well then." He sounded hesitant. "She's owed for the whole of the month."

An instant before he spoke, I understood why he'd led me to look at the calendar. I believe I blushed to discover that between brother and sister all was so frank and straightforward, everything spelled out in accounting terms. The explicit demand to pay up for the entire month was the thing that surprised me. I was also uncertain that I really owed anything. I hadn't kept my accounts with much precision during my relations with Felicita. Hadn't I always paid in advance, and wasn't I therefore already paid up for that portion of the month? I backed away, somewhat troubled, studying those peculiar eyes to ascertain whether they were begging or threatening. It's quite typical of a man of long and considerable experience like myself to be uncertain how to behave, aware that the most unexpected things may result from a mere word or action. You just have to consult the history of the world to know how causes and effects can assume the strangest relations. While I hesitated, I withdrew my wallet and began to count, paying attention not to mistake a five-hundred-lire note for a hundred-lire one. And after I'd counted them, I handed them over. The thing was done while I thought I was just keeping busy to gain time. "In the meantime I'll pay, and then I'll think," I said to myself.

But Felicita's brother gave the matter no more thought, indeed his eye ceased to scrutinize me and lost all its gleam. He put the money into a different pocket from the one with the 160 lire. Accounts and earnings in separate pockets. "Good day, sir," he said, and left. But soon he was back because he'd left behind on a chair another parcel similar to the one he'd brought me. By way of apology for returning, he said, "It's another hundred packs of Sports that I must deliver to another gentleman."

They were for poor Misceli, of course, who couldn't stand Sports either. I, however, smoked all of mine, apart from a few packs that I gave to my driver Fortunato. When I've paid for something, sooner or later I end up using it. It shows the principle of thrift in me. Every time I had that straw taste in my mouth, I was vividly reminded of Felicita and her brother. And being reminded so often, I came to be certain that I had not paid the woman's monthly allowance in advance. Having been convinced I'd been royally cheated, it was a great relief to find I'd only been made to pay an extra twenty days.

As I recall, I returned to see Felicita one more time before the twenty days expired, on account of that principle of thrift that had made me consume the Sports. "Well, now that I've paid," I said to myself, "I'd like to risk suggesting to my organism which way to fall. Just once! It will never notice I'm taking advantage of the occasion."

Just as I was about to ring the bell, the door to her quarters swung open. In the darkness, to my surprise, I saw her pretty, pale little face capped in a red bonnet that covered her head, her ears, and the nape of her neck. One blond curl, just one, had escaped from the hat onto her forehead. I knew this was about the time she went out every day to supervise the commercial transactions at her tobacco concession. I'd hoped to persuade her to delay for that modest amount of time I would need.

She didn't recognize me right away in the gloom. She said a name, neither mine nor Misceli's, in the form of a question, but I didn't hear her clearly. When she did see it was me, she gave me her hand quite nicely and without rancor, but she seemed curious. I held her icy little hand in both of mine, and then grew impetuous. She allowed her hand to rest inert in mine, but drew her head back. Never had that pin around which she was built leaned so far backwards, so far that I was tempted to let go of her hand and grab her around the waist, if only to hold her upright.

That distant face adorned by the one curl looked at me. Or did it look at me? Wasn't she perhaps looking at a problem in need of a rapid solution, immediately, right there on the stairs?

"It's impossible right now," she said after a long pause. She looked at me again. Then all her hesitation vanished. Her little figure remained in that perilous pose, unmoving, her face pale and serious beneath her blond curl; but without any haste, as if animated by a solemn resolution, she withdrew her hand.

"Yes, it's impossible," she added. She repeated this so I'd think she was still working out whether there might be some way to please me, but beyond her words there was nothing else about her that suggested she was still contemplating the problem. She had already come to a firm decision.

"You might want to come back on the first of the month," she said, "if you can; and then I'll see ... I have to think about it."

It's just recently, only since I put down this story of my affair with Felicita, that I've gained enough objectivity to judge her and myself fairly. I'd come to assert my right to those few days that remained of my subscription. She was letting me know that when I had declined to come on my assigned day I'd given up that right. I think if she'd proposed I pay to open a new subscription immediately, I'd have suffered less. I'm sure I wouldn't have run off. At that moment I was set on love, and a man of my age is like a crocodile on dry land; it needs, they say, considerable time to change direction. I would have paid right off for the whole month, merely to have her one last time.

But this made me quite indignant. Words escaped me; even the air seemed too scarce. "Ugh," I said in full fury. Believing I'd said something, I even stood waiting for a moment, as if I expected that my "ugh," a cry to wound her and express all my deepest discontent, would elicit a reply from her. But neither she nor I said another word. I started down the stairs. A few steps down I stopped and turned to look at her. Maybe that pallid face of hers would now reveal that her egoism wasn't so ruthless, her calculation not so cold. But I could not see her face. She had turned, intent on getting the key in the lock to close her quarters, destined to remain empty for several hours. Again I said "Ugh," but not so loud that she would hear me. I said it to the world, to society, to our institutions and to Mother Nature, all of whom had conspired to allow me to find myself on those stairs and in that position.

It was my last love. Now that the whole adventure has settled into the frame of the past, I no longer consider it terribly unworthy, because Felicita, her blond hair and pale face, her fine nose and enigmatic eyes, her spare words that only once in a while revealed how icy her heart was—well, she's a woman one can regret. But after her, there was no place for other loves. She taught me. Before her, when by chance I spent more than ten minutes in the presence of a woman, I'd feel desire and hope surging in my heart. Of course I wanted to conceal both, but even more, I wanted them to blossom, to feel life more intensely and that I was part of it. To allow desire and hope to blossom, I could only clothe them in words and reveal them. How many times I was laughed at! I am now condemned to play the very old man; Felicita taught me that. In love, I have learned, I am not worth more than what I pay.

And I'm always aware how unattractive I am. Just this morning, on rising, I thought about the position of my mouth at the moment I opened my eyes. My lower jaw sagged on the side that lay on the pillow, and my tongue, stiff and swollen, hung out.

Immediately I thought of Felicita, whom I very often recall with desire and acrimony. And I murmured, "The damn thing was right!"

"What damn thing?" asked Augusta, who was getting dressed.

"A certain Misceli I happened to meet was right, when he said he could not understand why we are born, live, and grow old," I replied promptly.

In this way I told her everything without compromising myself in the least.

To date, no one has taken Felicita's place. Nevertheless I'm still trying to fool Mother Nature, who's keeping an eye out to suppress me as soon as it's evident I'm no longer fit to reproduce. Every day I take a little of that medicine, dosing it advisedly in just the quantities Hahnemann counseled. I watch women go by, I follow their footsteps hoping to see in those legs something other than a device for walking, and to feel the desire to stop them and stroke them. The dosage, however, is even stingier than Hahnemann and I would like. I must keep watch over my eyes so they don't reveal what they're looking for, so as you can imagine, the medicine hardly ever works. You can do without someone caressing you and still feel something, but you cannot pretend absolute indifference without the risk that it will chill your soul. And having written this, I now understand better my adventure with old Signora Dondi. I bowed to her in order to have something to do, and to savor her beauty. It's an old man's destiny to make nice bows.

Now you mustn't think that fleeting relations, motivated only by the desire to escape death, don't leave traces, don't brighten or disturb life every bit as much as the one with Carla, or that with Felicita. Sometimes—rarely—they even leave an indelible memory, on account of the powerful impression they make. I remember a young woman seated across from me on the tram. She certainly left me with memories. We had arrived at a certain intimacy, because I gave her a name: Amphora. Her face was not especially beautiful but her eyes were very lively, rather round, and observed everything with great curiosity and a slightly childish shrewdness. She might even have been more than twenty years old, but I wouldn't have been surprised to see her, for fun, quietly grab the little pigtails of a girl who happened to be sitting beside her and give them a yank. Whether because she had an exceptional form, or because of the effect produced by her dress, her torso, though slight, resembled an elegant amphora posed on her hips. I very much admired her torso, and to cheat Mother Nature, who had her eye on me I thought, "You see, I do not have to die yet, because if this child were to wish it, I would be ready and willing to procreate."

My face must have taken on an odd look while I was gazing at the amphora. But it wasn't lechery; what I was thinking about was death. Others, though, saw desire in me. And when she got down from the tram, I realized that the girl, most likely from a well-to-do family, was accompanied by an elderly woman, a chaperone. And this woman, as she passed me, looked me in the eye and hissed, "You old satyr." Old, she called me. To mention it was to provoke death. "You old fool," I said. But she went on her way without a saying another word.

FOREWORD

(These are the opening pages of the novel that Italo Svevo started writing in the summer of 1928.)

IT HAPPENED this year, in an April that brought us one foggy, rainy day after another, briefly interrupted by startling patches of sunshine and even warmth.

I was in the car heading home with Augusta after a short outing to Capodistria. My eyes had tired of the sun, and I needed rest. Not sleep, just absence of movement. I felt far away from the things around me, but nevertheless I allowed them in, because there was nothing else to see, and they slipped by, meaningless. Everything had become colorless after sundown, and the green fields were overtaken by gray houses and squalid lanes so familiar it was as if we'd seen them before, and looking at them was not much different from sleeping.

In Piazza Goldoni we were stopped by the traffic police, and I came to. I saw a very young girl come toward us and, in order to avoid the other cars, approach our vehicle close enough to brush against it, a girl dressed in white with green ribbons at her neck, and green stripes on a light cape, open, partly covering her dress, also white, and marked at intervals like the cape, with slender stripes of that luminous green. She was such a vigorous affirmation of the season. A beautiful young girl! She smiled in the face of the evident danger, and her large dark eyes, widening, observed and measured. The smile revealed how white her teeth were in contrast to her rosy skin. She held her hands close to her chest in an effort to make herself small, and in one of them she held a pair of soft gloves. My eyes focused on those hands, their shape and their whiteness, long fingers and tiny palms that smoothly joined her plump wrists.

I have no idea why, just then, I felt it would be cruel if the moment slipped by without any connection being forged between the young lady and me. Very cruel. Something had to be done in haste, but haste creates confusion. But then I remembered! There was already a connection between us. I knew her. I bowed in her direction, leaning forward toward the windscreen so as to be visible, and smiled, a smile meant to communicate my admiration for her courage and her youth. However, I soon quit smiling, having remembered I was showing off how much gold I had in my mouth, and just gazed at her, intent and serious. The girl had time to look at me curiously, and she replied to my bow with a hesitant wave that lent a remorseful look to her face, which had lost its smile and its light, as if between my eyes and her form a prism had deflected it.

Augusta raised her lorgnette to her eyes immediately, fearing she would see the young lady end up under the wheels of the car. She signaled hello to the girl so I would not be conspicuously alone in greeting her, and then asked me, "Who's that young woman?"

I couldn't quite remember her name. I gazed into the past, fiercely hoping to find it, flipping rapidly from year to year, going far, far back. When I found her, she was by the side of a friend of my father's. "Old Dondi's daughter," I muttered uncertainly. Now that I had said the name, I seemed to recollect better. The memory of the girl brought with it that of a small, green garden around a little villa. And there was more: a memory of something she'd said that made everyone there laugh. "Why does one cat never fall from a roof, why always two?" Thus she revealed her brazen ignorance to all, just as now in Piazza Goldoni, and I, too, was so innocent that I laughed along with the others, rather than take her, so beautiful and so very desirable, in my arms. You know, that memory rejuvenated me for a moment, and I recalled I'd once been capable of grabbing, holding on, fighting.

This reverie was brusquely interrupted when Augusta burst out laughing. "Old Dondi's daughter is your age now. So who was that you were bowing to? The Signorina Dondi is six years older than me. Ha! If it had been her, she'd have been limping and tottering and might have fallen right under the wheels, not like that young thing smiling in the face of danger."

Once again the light of this world shifted, as if it were suddenly coming to me through a prism. I didn't laugh along with Augusta right away. But I knew I must! Otherwise I'd reveal how much the adventure had meant to me, and I had never once confessed it to Augusta.

"Yes, you're right, I didn't think of that. Every day everything changes a little, and it adds up to a lot in a year—and a very great deal in seventy." Then I said something that was quite sincere. Rubbing my eyes the way one does after sleep, I added, "I was forgetting that I'm old myself, and therefore all my contemporaries are old too. Even those I haven't seen aging, even those who don't show themselves in public and never provoke any gossip, whom nobody has been observing, still grow older every day." I was beginning to sound childish in my efforts to conceal that flash of youth that had been granted to me. It was time to change my tone, and trying to sound more carefree, I inquired, "Where does old Dondi's daughter live now?" Augusta didn't know. She hadn't come back to Trieste since marrying a foreigner.

Now I saw poor old Signora Dondi, in her skirts that had remained long all these years, far away in some remote corner of the earth, a stranger among people who had not known her as a girl. I was moved, because that was my fate too, although I had never left home. Augusta alone claims to remember me perfectly, with all my great youthful qualities, and a few defects, primarily a fear of aging that she still hasn't forgiven, it being evident to this day that I suffer from it. But I don't believe her. I scarcely remember anything about her beyond what I see in front of me. In fact, she knew only a part of my youthful days; I mean she knew them quite superficially. I myself remember my adventures in those times better than I do what she looked like or her feelings. There are odd moments when youth seems to have returned, and I have to run to the mirror to settle my accounts with time. It's by looking at the line of my chin so badly deformed by ropes of excess skin, that I bring myself back to my place. Once I told my nephew Carlo—who's a medical man, and young, and therefore knows all about old age—of these fantasies of youth that I have from time to time. Carlo flashed an impish smile and told me that this was a sure symptom of old age, because I had completely forgotten what it was like to be young, and had to study the flesh under my chin to refresh my memory. He then laughed a resounding laugh and added, "It's like your neighbor, old Cralli, who sincerely believes he's the father of that child his young wife's about to bear."

No, it's not! I'm still young enough not to make such mistakes. It's just that I don't know how to move back and forth in time well. And I don't think it's entirely my fault. I'm sure of it, although I'd never dare to say so to Carlo, who wouldn't understand and would mock me. Time performs its devastation cruelly and firmly, then marches by in an orderly procession of days, months, and years, and when it is far enough away to disappear from sight, the order dissolves. And every hour it seeks its place in some other day, and every day in some other year. And thus, in memory, one year appears sunlit, like a long summer, while another is all racked with chills. And especially chilly and dark is that year when you can remember nothing in its right place: three hundred and sixty-five days each of twenty-four dead, ruined hours. A slaughter.

At times, a light flares in those dead years, illuminating some episode of your life that reveals itself a rare flower, of a powerful perfume. Thus I was never so close to the Signorina Dondi as on that day in Piazza Goldoni. In that garden of the villa (how many years ago?) I scarcely saw her, and being so young when I passed by her, I didn't appreciate her grace and innocence. Now, as I catch up with her, the others begin to laugh, seeing us together. Why didn't I see her, why didn't I understand sooner? Perhaps in the present, everything is shadowed by our worries, by the dangers looming over us? And perhaps that's something we never see, never hear, except when far away, safe and sound.

But here in my room I am immediately safe and sound, and I can collect these pages to study and analyze the present in its incomparable light, and take hold of that part of the past that hasn't yet vanished.

So I shall take down the present and that part of the past that hasn't yet vanished, not to keep it in my memory, but to concentrate my mind. Had I done so before I'd have been less shocked and upset by that encounter in Piazza Goldoni. I wouldn't have simply stared at that girl like a man whose eyes are protected by God. From head to foot.

I don't feel old but I have the impression I'm rusty. I have to think and write in order to feel alive, because the life I lead—what with the considerable virtue I possess and which is attributed to me, and my many affections and duties that bind and paralyze me—deprives me of my every liberty. I live with the same inertia as the dead. I want to shake myself, arise. Perhaps I'll even become more virtuous, more affectionate. Maybe even passionately virtuous, but of a virtue that is truly my own, not that virtue preached by others which, when I wear it, oppresses rather than dresses me. I'll abandon that clothing, or I'll know how to mold it to me.

My writing, then, will be a hygienic measure to be undertaken every evening just before I take my purgative. And I hope these pages will also be marked with words I normally do not use, for only then will the cure be effective.

Once before, I took to writing with the same promise to tell the truth, and that time, too, it was a hygienic exercise, because it was supposed to ready me for a psychoanalytic cure. The cure failed, but the pages remained. How precious they are! Yesterday I reread them. I feel that the part of my life described there is the only part I have lived. I didn't find old Signora Dondi (Emma, yes, Emma), but I discovered many other things. Even a very important event, which isn't told but hinted at by an empty space it fits into perfectly. I would record it immediately if right now I had not forgotten what it was. But it won't be lost, for surely when I reread the pages, it will reappear. And they are there, always at my disposal, safe from chaos. Time has been crystallized, and can be recovered if one knows how to open the appropriate page. Like a railroad timetable.

Now, certainly, everything I write about I did, but when I read it the story seems more important than my life, which I think of as long and empty. Of course, when one writes about one's life one makes it sound more serious than it actually was. Life itself is diluted, and therefore partly obfuscated by the many things that are never mentioned in an account. You don't write of breathing until it becomes breathlessness, nor of holidays, meals, or sleep, unless for some tragic reason they are wanting. While in reality they happen along with many other things, with pendulum-like regularity, imperiously occupying so much of your day that there's no time to laugh or cry excessively. For this reason alone, an account of a life, from which a great part, that which everyone knows about and nobody speaks about, is missing, will be far more intense than life itself.

In short, life is idealized in the telling, and now I'm preparing to take on this task a second time, quivering as if I were approaching some sacred thing. Who knows whether the present, attentively observed, will turn up some stretch of my youth that my legs are now too weary to walk and that I'll beckon to return to me. Even in the few lines I've put down I can see it; it invades me, so that the weariness of age grows easier in my veins.

There is one great difference between the state of mind in which I told my life the first time, and this one. My situation has grown simpler. I continue to struggle between past and present, but at least hope doesn't try to come into it, that anxious hope that belongs to the future. And so I continue to live in a composite time, as humans are destined to do, although their grammar is made of pure tenses that seem to be made for the animal world, where the beasts, when they are not afraid, live happily in a crystalline present. But for the venerable, the very old man (for I am a very old man: this is the first time I announce it and the first conquest I owe to my new powers of concentration) that mutilation in which life loses something it never had—the future—certainly simplifies our lives, but also renders them so senseless that I might be tempted to use the brief present to tear out the few hairs remaining on this crooked head.

I, however, insist on doing something else in that present time, and if, as I hope, there's room to accomplish something, I'll know for sure that it's larger than it seems. It's difficult to measure, and the mathematician who seeks to do so will err badly and supply the proof it's not a job for him. I believe I know at least how one should go about measuring the thing. When memory has removed from life's events anything in them that could evoke surprise, fear, or chaos, we can say they have moved into the past.

I've considered this problem for so long that even my inert life has offered me the occasion to test my ideas, if someone else were interested in repeating the experiment with more precise instruments—someone with more instruction than I have, and better tools.

One day last spring Augusta and I gathered our courage and drove all the way to Udine to have luncheon at a celebrated tavern where the slow and perfect art of cooking on the spit is still practiced. We then drove on toward Carnia to see the great mountains close up. Soon we were attacked by the weariness of the old, that fatigue that comes from the inertia of too much comfort. We got out of the car, and feeling a powerful need to stretch our legs, climbed a small wooded hill that rose next to the main road. Up there we were awarded a pleasant surprise. We could no longer see the road nor the fields at the foot of the mount we'd come up, but only innumerable sweet green hills that stood before some enormous nearby mountains peaked with blue rock, observing us very gravely. On foot we'd managed to find new vistas more easily than with the car, and I was deeply pleased and felt a joy I'll never forget. A joy due to the surprise, or to the gentle sweet air free of the dust of the road, or to the fact we were completely alone here? Joy made me enterprising, and from those heights I managed to get to the other side of the hill, opposite the road we'd driven in on. The path, marked in the tall grass, was easy. Looking down I saw a house at the foot of the hill, and in front of it a man who was bending a piece of iron on an anvil with vigorous blows of a hammer. Like a child I listened in wonder to the metallic ring of that anvil, which arrived at my ear when the hammer had already been raised to strike a new blow. Yes, I was a child, but Mother Nature had her infantile side too, inventing that pronounced contrast between sight and sound.

For a long time after, I would remember the joy of those colors, and the fact that no one was there but us, and also the dispute between my eye and my ear. But then memory's seriousness and the mind's logic intervened to correct nature's disorder, and today when I think of that hammer, as I see it strike the anvil, I hear the sound it provokes at the same moment. The performance falsifies itself in part. The disorder of the past takes over from the disorder of the present. That family of hills grew more numerous, and they all became more thickly wooded. The stone of the mountains became darker and more somber, perhaps drew even closer to us, but everything was proportionate and harmonic. The pity is that I didn't take note of how many days that present needed to transform itself into past. And even if I had taken note, I could only have said: In the mind of Zeno Cosini, seventy years old, things mature in many hours and in many minutes. How many other experiences, of the greatest variety of individuals, at their most various ages, would have to be surveyed to arrive at the general law fixing the frontier between the present and the past!

And so I'll end my life with a notebook in hand like my deceased father. How I laughed at that book! Even now I smile thinking of how he dedicated it to the future. He kept notes of his duties, his visits, and so forth. Anyway, I also possess a notebook. Many of the notes in it begin with exhortations: don't forget to do such and such on such and such a day. He had faith in them, the exhortations buried in that notebook of his. But I have proof that his faith was misplaced. I found one that read, "I must *absolutely*"—the word is underlined—"not forget to tell Olivi when I have the opportunity that upon my death my son must be made to appear to all as master of the firm, although he shall never be such."

I suppose the opportunity to speak with Olivi never presented itself. But of course any effort to move from one time, one tense, to another is futile, and only an ingenuous soul like my father could imagine he could determine his own future. Perhaps time doesn't exist, as the philosophers tell us, but the recipients that contain it certainly do, and they are almost perfectly sealed. Only a few drops pass from one to another.

I'd like to look around me now and gather this memorable day together, sending the hour during which I write on to tomorrow. Of my handsome, comfortable study many times redecorated by Augusta over the years, causing me great inconvenience while never introducing any real novelty, I have little to say. It is more or less as it was just after we were married, and I've already described it once. There's recently been a truly distressing change. My violin disappeared from its place a few days ago, along with the music stand. Although it's true that the gramophone thus conquered the position it needed to broadcast its voice more vigorously. I bought the gramophone a year ago, and it was expensive, and so are the records I'm always buying. I don't regret the expense, but I would have liked to leave the violin in its place. I haven't touched it for nearly two years. In my hands it had become unsteady and careless of rhythm, and I seemed to be losing my touch. But I loved to see it there in its place awaiting better times, while Augusta didn't understand why it should take up space in my room. There are some things she doesn't understand, and I cannot explain them to her. And one day, pressed by her mania to impose order, she took it away, assuring me that I merely had to ask and she would give it back to me in a moment. However, I will certainly never ask, though it's not at all certain that, had it remained where it was, I might not someday have taken it in hand. The decision I would now have to make is altogether different. I would have to beg Augusta to bring it back, with the promise I would play it as soon as she did. But I'm incapable of contracting such long-term obligations. And so here I am, decisively cut off from another aspect of my youth. Augusta still hasn't understood how much care one must take in dealing with an old man.

There would be nothing new in this room of mine if right now it weren't filled with sounds that have nothing to do with the gramophone. Twice a week (not on Sundays, but on Mondays and Saturdays) a music-loving wino comes up the steep path by my villa. At first I was annoyed, then amused, and finally I came to love him. I often watch him from my window, having turned out all the lights in the room, and observe him there on that path bleached white by the rays of the moon: small, slight, but standing tall, his lips raised to the heavens. He walks slowly, not because the path is difficult, but so that he can dedicate his full breath to the notes that he draws out so ardently. Sometimes he stops altogether, when he comes to a note that he's wary of singing because he thinks it is especially difficult. To me, the fact that his song is always the same is proof of the man's absolute innocence. Far from him any temptation to invent. At times he will hover on a certain pitch before sliding up or down to the accepted note. It's an essential part of his repertoire because it helps him center the note. Maybe he doesn't know he has altered the music, and loves it just as he sings it. He has no ambitions and therefore he lacks ill will. If I were to meet him coming along that path at night, knowing him a man of disinterested humanity, I wouldn't be afraid of him; I'd join him and ask his permission to sing along with him. His song is from *Un ballo in maschera*. He'd be very surprised if a cop ordered him to keep quiet. When he sings, *Alzati! La tua figlia a te concedo rivedere. Nell'ombra e nel silenzio là . . .* , he's truly speaking to Amelia.*

Of course there's quite bit of wine behind that music, but never did wine play a more noble part. My singer lives in that timeworn story. The tale's reborn for him twice a week, surprising and gripping as if it were new each time. How is he able every other evening to forego the wine that brings him such delight? What a model of moderation!

My driver Fortunato knows him. He tells me he's a carpenter who lives down below in a modest little house. He's married. He's not even forty years old, but he has a son of twenty. So he thinks of himself as old, and for him the past is even more distant than mine. How

* The words to the aria are reproduced as if by ear, without reference to the libretto. The actual lyrics are: *Alzati! là tuo figlio / A te concedo riveder. Nell'ombra / E nel silenzio, là* ("Arise! I permit you to see your son again. There, in the shadows and in silence"). He has misheard the first *là* ("there") as the feminine article *la*, and the son (*figlio*) thus becomes a daughter (*figlia*).

moral that man is! It took me a good seventy years to detach myself from the present. And I'm still not satisfied and try to get back there through these pages.

I won't ever try to get to know him. His faint voice seems to belong to faraway times. It provides emotion, being a lament in itself, and that state of disarray that follows an adventure. That solitary voice, and I here at my desk analyzing the hesitations and the ardor. A perfect order! The hours to come will never alter that voice for me. I'll look again at these notes the next time I hear him to see whether a new present will correct my memory and prove that I was wrong.

I'm tired of writing this evening. Augusta, who not long ago called to me from across the corridor, will have fallen asleep in her orderly bed, her head tied up in that netting fastened under her chin that she puts up with in order to tame her cropped gray hair. A vise, a weight, that would prevent me closing an eye.

She sleeps lightly, but more noisily than in the past. Especially in those first breaths, as she begins to abandon herself. It's as if all of a sudden other organs that were not ready were called on to carry out her respiration, and having been abruptly shaken out of sleep, make a lot of noise. This machine of ours is horrid when old. When I've heard Augusta's struggle I dread my own to come, and don't get to sleep unless I allow myself a double sleeping draft. So I do well not to turn in until Augusta is already asleep. It's true that I wake her, but she goes back to sleep much more quietly.

And here I suggest something to myself in imitation of my father: remember not to complain too much about old age in these pages. You may aggravate your situation.

Although it will be hard not to speak of it. I'm less ingenuous than my father; I know from the beginning that this is a suggestion made in vain. Being old all day long, without a moment of reprieve! And getting older every instant! It costs a lot of energy to accustom myself to how I am today, and tomorrow I'll have to impose the same toll to get myself back in a chair that's less comfortable every day. Who can deprive me of the right to talk about it, to shout and protest? Protest is in any case the shortest path to resignation.

TRANSLATOR'S AFTERWORD
Why Translate Svevo Again

ZENO COSINI, the narrator of *Il vegliardo* (*A Very Old Man*), has
been buying and selling during the war—profiteering, in short. The
conflict over, he has handed the day-to-day management of his company to his manager Olivi. Trieste is no longer an Austrian city, and
the new Italian government and its regulations flummox him. The
large shipment of soap he acquired as peace was approaching proves
a business disaster. It's a whole new world after the war, and he's too
lazy, too proud, not sharp enough or single-minded enough to make
his way in it. In the first story, "The Contract," we see him bullied
into ceding most of his firm to Olivi. Embarrassed, ashamed, he retires,
never to set foot in the business again. He's grown old (he's in his
sixties or seventies), a *vegliardo*.

His world narrowed to that of his family, he broods about Darwin
and heredity, and what his children, Alfio and Antonia, both disappointing in different ways, have inherited from him. Alfio, after a
postwar communist phase, has become a singularly unsuccessful
modern artist. Daughter Antonia, a paragon of virtue, has chosen
the dullest husband she could find, who then dies, leaving her to
become an impossibly irritating inconsolable widow. Wife Augusta
cares more for her birds than for anyone else, but they are a happy
enough old couple, despite his interlude with Felicita, his hardheaded
working-class mistress. The only family member he really enjoys is
his seven-year-old grandson, Umbertino, so wondrously new to life,
so unpredictable.

In this new era after the Great War, Zeno's life has shrunk drasti-
cally, and he studies his prison, his household, with irony, forbearance,

sometimes annoyance. He mopes about times past, decides that old age means living in "various tenses," and that memory, as recorded on paper, must mix its tenses too.

A Very Old Man reprises many themes dear to Svevo: ineptitude and inadaptation to middle-class life; aging; confession, deceit, and self-deception; the fragility and foolishness of the proper bourgeois gentleman and paterfamilias. The psychology of these tales remains startlingly evocative today, although they are clearly set in a now distant time and place: around the Great War, in the onetime Habsburg city of Trieste on the Adriatic.

THE TRANSLATION STRATEGY

Svevo's style is relatively simple and often colloquial in flavor, although the register varies and sometimes includes jargon from the business world where he spent so many years. Indeed, his style, especially that of his first novel *Una Vita* (*A Life*), was sharply criticized by some Italian critics, who detected an ugly, philistine use of "business Italian." It's not clear, however, whether these readers entirely distinguished between Svevo's own sense of language and the language that he uses sarcastically, or to shed light on character. The simplicity of his sentences was, besides, at odds with the ornate, clause-upon-clause style that was still popular in much literary Italian when he began writing.

It is true, however, that written Italian was a secondary conquest for Svevo. As he himself recalled in his autobiographical writings, his native tongue was the Triestine dialect, an almost entirely spoken idiom, more direct and rapid-paced than Italian. It was not until an English-speaking writer accustomed to a colloquial style and freer kind of syntax than Italians enjoyed—James Joyce—recognized that this, too, could be Italian literature, that Svevo's fiction began to get the hearing it deserved.

The anglophone translator, grappling with Svevo's irregular style, will not find it particularly awkward or oversimplified. The greatest challenge is another: to maintain the liveliness and colloquial nature of the prose while not falling back repeatedly on any particular English vernacular (American or British English, or a subspecies), which would tend to domesticate the Triestine setting of the fiction, making it falsely familiar. The Italian, nearly one hundred years old, was of its time, and it would be wrong to use "period" diction. It needs to be anchored in a register that isn't hypercontemporary but can sometimes sound more modern than the English version published in 1969. The reader will be reminded that the story is set in another time and place if the register is relatively colloquial: not too literary but not too informal. The British figures of speech and idioms running through the fragments of *Il vegliardo* translated by Ben Johnson and P. N. Furbank (as *The Further Confessions of Zeno*) have aged, and lend an unjustified "vintage" flavor.

My second goal was to avoid the awkwardness of translationese, the mindless repetition of Italian sentence structures in English that makes a text sound alien. (I don't agree with the school that holds that this is a way to preserve the foreignness of a text; to my mind, foreignizing must be achieved mainly at the level of language and content.)

A typical Italian syntactic formula is the use of nouns to describe what in English would be conveyed with verbs. Nouns, often abstract ones, are coupled with weak verbs like "to be" or "to have". Italians write: *Avevo la convinzione*, "I had the conviction"; in English, barring some special circumstance, one ordinarily writes "I was convinced." The second sounds more concrete, more English. So when Svevo writes *traspariva la mia convinzione*, I have translated it as "you could see I expected..." The 1969 translation also converts the noun to a verb, but it is unnecessarily wordy: "one could read between the lines that I imagined..."

A final consideration was the music, or the rhythm, of the original. Svevo's colloquial prose has a distinct rhythm that was has often been spoiled in translation. The effort to be faithful to the original can produce wordy patches and awkward sentences. These need to be reworked in order to reproduce the concise and humorous tone of the Italian. Bringing out the humor in *Il vegliardo* involves tinkering both with the timing and the language.

ARGUMENT FOR A RETRANSLATION

The five fragments that make up the unfinished novel are usually called, as Svevo himself did in his notes, *Il vegliardo*—"venerable" but also "tottering," an old man still hanging on, an ambiguity difficult to convey in a single English word. In English, this first became *The Further Confessions of Zeno*, attractive to booksellers, but probably not a title the author of *Una Vita* and *Senilità* would have conceived.

Another false step in the earlier translation is its repetition of French words—*grippe, fils*—which, when employed in English, give a mistakenly elevated tone. Here Zeno, if he were speaking English, would say "flu" and "son." When an event *era da perdere i sensi*, the previous translator writes "enough to make you go mad," but Svevo says "it's enough to make you faint," or "it's enough to make your head spin," a much livelier phrase. *Il freddo e lo sconforto* doesn't mean "the chill and the discomfort," but rather "the cold and my dejection," being a typical colloquialism not appreciated in writing.

Svevo introduces the elderly Zeno Cosini by signaling his informal voice immediately. The second sentence begins "*C'è mio nipote Carlo, che,*" "There's my nephew Carlo, who..." The 1969 translation smooths over this locution: "My doctor nephew Carlo, whom I consulted." My solution: "There's my nephew Carlo—I talked it over with him." This problem of tone arises again and again in Johnson and Furbank's version.

They also make errors of interpretation, which often flatten or banalize Svevo's vivacity. Here are a few: After the Italian takeover of Trieste, Svevo writes of *le truppe austriache e l'inedia austriaca*, which is translated as "Austrian soldiers and short rations," when *inedia* here means "lassitude," "indolence." The phrase *dall'imo delle mie viscere* has been translated with the banal "from the depths of my soul," when the word *viscere*, meaning "intestines," is used—the "rowdy voice" is, rather, "howling at me from deep in my gut." The story Svevo entitled "Il mio ozio" (after the Latin *otium*) is also misleadingly called "Indolence," when "My Leisure" is what was intended. The previous translation also has Zeno at one point calling himself a "war profiteer," when the text merely speaks of "war commerce." Profiteering is Olivi's accusation; to put the word in Cosini's mouth is a serious error in point of view.

But the biggest failing of the previous translation is its inability to capture the succinctness and rhythm of Svevo's prose. Timing and the element of surprise make Svevo's text witty; the same is not always true of Johnson and Furbank. When Zeno writes a letter to his former business manager, *Gli scrivevo che il destino aveva voluto ciò che il mio povero padre aveva escluso cioè che divenissi il padrone dei miei affari.* The Johnson version: "I said that destiny had so willed it that the possibility my father had ruled out had actually been realised: I had become the master of my own business." My wording aims to sound more like Svevo's Italian: "Fate, I wrote, had decreed just what my poor father had deemed impossible: that I should become the master of my own affairs."

—FREDERIKA RANDALL

OTHER NEW YORK REVIEW CLASSICS

For a complete list of titles, visit www.nyrb.com.